TOM SAWYER ABROAD

CHILDREN'S
CLASSICS

TOM SAWYER ABROAD

Mark Twain

Bloomsbury Books
London

This edition published 1994 by Bloomsbury Books, an
imprint of The Godfrey Cave Group, 42 Bloomsbury Street,
London, WC1B 3QJ.

ISBN 1 85471 223 3

Printed and bound by Firmin-Didot (France),
Group Herissey. No d'impression : 27839.

Contents

1

Tom Seeks New Adventures

Do you reckon Tom Sawyer was satisfied after all them adventures? I mean the adventures we had down the river, and the time we set the slave Jim free and Tom got shot in the leg. No, he wasn't. It only just p'isoned him for more. That was all the effect it had. You see, when we three came back up the river in glory, as you may say, from that long travel, and the village received us with a torchlight procession and speeches, and everybody hurrah'd and shouted, it made us heroes, and that was what Tom Sawyer had always been hankering to be.

For a while he was satisfied. Everybody made much of him, and he tilted up his nose and stepped around the town as though he owned it.

Some called him Tom Sawyer the traveller, and that just swelled him up fit to bust. You see he laid over me and Jim considerable, because we only went down the river on a raft and came back by the steamboat, but Tom went by the steamboat both ways. The boys envied me and Jim a good deal, but land! They just knuckled to the dirt before TOM.

Well, I don't know; maybe he might have been satisfied if it hadn't been for old Nat Parsons, which was postmaster, and powerful long and slim, and kind o' good-hearted and silly, and bald-headed, on account of his age, and about the talkiest old cretur I ever see. For as much as thirty years he'd been the only man in the village that had a reputation—I mean a reputation for being a traveller, and of course he was mortal proud of it, and it was reckoned that in the course of that thirty years he had told about that journey over a million times and enjoyed it every time. And now comes along a boy not quite fifteen, and sets everybody admiring and gawking over his travels, and it just give the poor old man the high strikes. It made him sick to listen to Tom, and to hear the people say "My

land!" "Did you ever!" "My goodness sakes
alive!" and all such things, but he couldn't pull
away from it, any more than a fly that's got its
hind leg fast in the molasses. And always when
Tom come to a rest, the poor old cretur would
chip in on his same old travels and work them
for all they were worth; but they were pretty
faded, and didn't go for much, and it was pitiful
to see. And then Tom would take another in-
nings, and then the old man again—and so on,
and so on, for an hour and more, each trying to
beat out the other.

You see, Parsons' travels happened like this:
When he first got to be postmaster and was
green in the business, there come a letter for
somebody he didn't know, and there wasn't any
such person in the village. Well, he didn't know
what to do, nor how to act, and there the letter
stayed, and stayed, week in and week out, till the
bare sight of it gave him a conniption. The post-
age wasn't paid on it, and that was another thing
to worry about. There wasn't any way to collect
that ten cents, and he reckoned the gov'ment
would hold him responsible for it and maybe
turn him out besides, when they found he hadn't

collected it. Well, at last he couldn't stand it any longer. He couldn't sleep nights, he couldn't eat, he was thinned down to a shadder, yet he dasn't ask anybody's advice, for the very person he asked for advice might go back on him and let the gov'ment know about the letter. He had the letter buried under the floor, but that did no good; if he happened to see a person standing over the place it'd give him the cold shivers, and loaded him up with suspicions, and he would sit up that night till the town was still and dark, and then he would sneak there and get it out and bury it in another place. Of course, people got to avoiding him and shaking their heads and whispering, because, the way he was looking and acting, they judged he had killed somebody or done something terrible, they didn't know what, and if he had been a stranger they would've lynched him.

Well, as I was saying, it got so he couldn't stand it any longer; so he made up his mind to pull out for Washington, and just go to the President of the United States and make a clean breast of the whole thing, not keeping back an atom, and then fetch the letter out and lay it be-

fore the whole gov'ment, and say, "Now, there
she is—do with me what you're a mind to;
though as heaven is my judge I am an innocent
man and not deserving of the full penalties of
the law and leaving behind me a family that
must starve and yet hadn't a thing to do with it,
which is the whole truth and I can swear to it."

So he did it. He had a little wee bit of
steamboating, and some stagecoaching, but all
the rest of the way was horseback, and it took
him three weeks to get to Washington. He saw
lots of land and lots of villages and four cities.
He was gone 'most eight weeks, and there never
was such a proud man in the village as when he
got back. His travels made him the greatest man
in all that region, and the most talked about; and
people come from as much as thirty miles back
in the country, and from over in the Illinois bot-
toms, too, just to look at him—and there they'd
stand and gawk, and he'd gabble. You never
seen anything like it.

Well, there wasn't any way now to settle
which was the greatest traveller; some said it
was Nat, some said it was Tom. Everybody allowed that Nat had seen the most longitude, but

they had to give in that whatever Tom was short in longitude he had made up in latitude and climate. It was about a standoff; so both of them had to whoop up their dangerous adventures, and try to get ahead that way. That bullet wound in Tom's leg was a tough thing for Nat Parsons to buck against, but he bucked the best he could; and at a disadvantage, too, for Tom didn't set still as he'd orter done, to be fair, but always got up and sauntered around and worked his limp while Nat was painting up the adventure that he had in Washington; for Tom never let go that limp when his leg got well, but practised it nights at home, and kept it good as new right along.

Nat's adventure was like this; I don't know how true it is: maybe he got it out of a paper, or somewhere, but I will say this for him, that he did know how to tell it. He could make anybody's flesh crawl, and he'd turn pale and hold his breath when he told it, and sometimes women and girls got so faint they couldn't stick it out. Well, it was this way, as near as I can remember:

He come a-loping into Washington, and put up

his horse and shoved out to the President's house with his letter, and they told him the President was up to the Capitol, and just going to start for Philadelphia—not a minute to lose if he wanted to catch him. Nat 'most dropped, it made him so sick. His horse was put up, and he didn't know what to do. But just then along comes a man driving an old ramshackly hack, and he sees his chance. He rushes out and shouts, "A half a dollar if you git me to the Capitol in half an hour, and a quarter extra if you do it in twenty minutes!"

"Done!" says the man.

Nat he jumped in and slammed the door, and away they went a-ripping and a-tearing over the roughest road a body ever see, and the racket of it was something awful. Nat passed his arms through the loops and hung on for life and death, but pretty soon the hack hit a rock and flew up in the air, and the bottom fell out, and when it come down Nat's feet was on the ground, and he sees he was in the most desperate danger if he couldn't keep up with the hack. He was horrible scared, but he laid into his work for all he was worth, and hung tight to the arm loops and made his legs fairly fly. He yelled and shouted to the driver to stop, and so did the crowds along the street, for they could see his legs spinning under the coach, and his head and shoulders bobbing inside through the windows, and he was in awful danger; but the more they all shouted the more the driver whooped and yelled and lashed the horses and shouted, "Don't you fret, I's gwine to git you dah in time, boss; I's gwine to do it, sho'!" for you see he thought they were all hurrying him up, and, of course, he couldn't hear anything for the racket he was making. And so they went ripping along, and everybody just petrified to see it; and when they got to the Capitol at last it was the quickest trip that ever was made, and everybody said so. The horses laid down, and Nat dropped, all tuckered out, and he was all dust and rags and barefooted; but he was in time and just in time, and caught the President and give him the letter, and everything was all right, and the President give him a free pardon on the spot, and Nat give the driver two extra quarters instead of one, because he could see that if he hadn't had the hack he wouldn't a' got there in time, nor anywhere near it.

It was a powerful good adventure, and Tom Sawyer had to work his bullet wound mighty lively to hold his own against it.

Well, by and by Tom's glory got to paling down gradu'ly, on account of other things turning up for the people to talk about—first a horse race, and on top of that a house afire, and on top of that the circus, and on top of that the eclipse; and that started a revival, same as it always does, and by that time there wasn't any more talk about Tom, so to speak, and you never see a person so sick and disgusted.

Pretty soon he got to worrying and fretting right along day in and day out, and when I asked him what was he in such a state about, he said it 'most broke his heart to think how time was slipping away, and him getting older and older, and no wars breaking out and no way of making a name for himself that he could see. Now that is the way boys is always thinking, but he was the first one I ever heard come out and say it.

So then he set to work to get up a plan to make him celebrated; and pretty soon he struck it, and offered to take me and Jim in. Tom Sawyer was always free and generous that way. There's aplenty of boys that's mighty good and friendly when you've got a good thing, but when a good thing happens to come their way they don't say a word to you, and try to hog it all. That warn't ever Tom Sawyer's way, I can say that for him. There's plenty of boys that will come hankering and grovelling around you when you've got an apple and beg the core off of you; but when they've got one, and you beg for the core and re-mind them how you give them a core one time, they say thank you 'most to death, but there ain't a-going to be no core. But I notice they always git come up with; all you got to do is to wait.

Well, we went out in the woods on the hill, and Tom told us what it was. It was a crusade.

"What's a crusade?" I says.

He looked scornful, the way he's always done when he was ashamed of a person, and says:

"Huck Finn, do you mean to tell me you don't know what a crusade is."

"No," says I, "I don't. And I don't care to, nuther. I've lived till now and done without it, and had my health, too. But as soon as you tell me, I'll know, and that's soon enough. I don't see any use in finding out things and clogging up my head with them when I mayn't ever have any occasion to use 'em. There was Lance Williams, he learned how to talk Choctaw here till one come and dug his grave for him. Now, then, what's a crusade? But I can tell you one thing before you begin; if it's a patent right, there's no money in it. Bill Thompson he—"

"Patent right!" says he. "I never see such an idiot. Why, a crusade is a kind of war."

I thought he must be losing his mind. But no, he was in real earnest, and went right on, perfectly ca'm.

"A crusade is a war to recover the Holy Land from the paynim."

"Which Holy Land?"

"Why, the Holy Land—there ain't but one."

"What do we want of it?"

"Why, can't you understand? It's in the hands of the paynim, and it's our duty to take it away from them."

"How did we come to let them git hold of it?"

"We didn't come to let them git hold of it. They always had it."

"Why, Tom, then it must belong to them, don't it?"

"Why, of course it does. Who said it didn't?"

I studied over it, but couldn't seem to git at the right of it, no way. I says:

"It's too many for me, Tom Sawyer. If I had a farm and it was mine, and another person wanted it, would it be right for him to—"

"Oh, shucks! You don't know enough to come in when it rains, Huck Finn. It ain't a farm, it's entirely different. You see, it's like this. They own the land, just the mere land, and that's all they do own; but it was our folks, our Jews and Christians, that made it holy, and so they haven't any business to be there defiling it. It's a shame, and we ought not to stand it a minute. We ought to march against them and take it away from them."

"Why, it does seem to me it's the most mixed-up thing I ever see! Now, if I had a farm and another person—"

"Don't I tell you it hasn't got anything to do with farming? Farming is business, just common lowdown business, that's all it is, it's all you can say for it; but this is higher, this is religious, and totally different."

"Religious to go and take the land away from people that owns it?"

"Certainly; it's always been considered so."

Jim he shook his head, and says:

"Mars Tom, I reckon dey's a mistake about it somers—dey mos' sholy is. I's religious myself, en I knows plenty religious people, but I hain't run across none dat acts like dat."

It made Tom hot, and he says:

"Well, it's enough to make a body sick, such mullet-headed ignorance! If either of you'd read anything about history, you'd know that Richard Cur de Loon, and the Pope, and Godfrey de Bulleyn, and lots more of the most noble-hearted and pious people in the world, hacked and hammered at the paynims for more than two hundred years trying to take their land away from them, and swum neck-deep in blood the whole time— and yet there's a couple of sap-headed country yahoos out in the backwoods of Missouri setting themselves up to know more about the rights and wrongs of it than they did! Talk about cheek!"

Well, of course, that put a more different light on it, and me and Jim felt pretty cheap and ignorant, and wished we hadn't been quite so chipper. I couldn't say nothing, and Jim he couldn't for a while; then he says:

"Well, den, I reckon it's all right; beca'se ef dey didn't know, dey ain't no use for po' ignorant folks like us to be trying to know; en so, ef it's our duty, we got to go en tackle it en do de bes' we can. Same time, I feel as sorry for dem paynims as Mars Tom. De hard part gwine to be to kill folks dat a body hain't been 'quainted wid and dat hain't done him no harm. Dat's it, you see. Ef we wus to go 'mongst 'em, jist we three, en say we's hungry, en ast 'em for a bite to eat, why maybe dey's jist like yuther people. Don't you reckon dey is? Why, dey'd give it, I know dey would, en den—"

"Then what?"

"Well, Mars Tom, my idea is like dis. It ain't no use, we can't kill dem po' strangers dat ain't doin' us no harm, till we've had practice—I knows it perfectly well, Mars Tom—'deed I knows it perfectly well. But ef we takes a' axe or two, jist you en me en Huck, en slips acrost de river tonight arter de moon's gone down, en kills dat sick fam'ly dat's over on the Sny, en burns dey house down, en—"

"Oh, you make me tired!" says Tom. "I don't want to argue any more with people like you and

Huck Finn, that's always wandering from the subject, and ain't got any more sense than to try to reason out a thing that's pure theology by the laws that protect real estate!"

Now that's just where Tom Sawyer warn't fair. Jim didn't mean no harm, and I didn't mean no harm. We knowed well enough that he was right and we was wrong, and all we was after was to get at the how of it, and that was all; and the only reason he couldn't explain it so we could understand it was because we was ignorant—yes, and pretty dull, too, I ain't denying that; but, land! That ain't no crime, I should think.

But he wouldn't hear no more about it—just said if we had tackled the thing in the proper spirit, he would 'a' raised a couple of thousand knights and put them in steel armour from head to heel, and made me a lieutenant and Jim a sutler, and took the command himself and brushed the whole paynim outfit into the sea like flies and come back across the world in a glory like sunset. But he said we didn't know enough to take the chance when we had it, and he wouldn't ever offer it again. And he didn't. When he once got set, you couldn't budge him.

But I didn't care much. I am peaceable, and don't get up rows with people that ain't doing nothing to me. I allowed if the paynim was satisfied I was, and we would let it stand at that.

Now Tom he got all that notion out of Walter Scott's book, which he was always reading. And it was a wild notion, because in my opinion he never could've raised the men, and if he did, as like as not he would've got licked. I took the book and read all about it, and as near as I could make it out, most of the folks that shook farming to go crusading had a mighty rocky time of it.

2

The Balloon Ascension

Well, Tom got up one thing after another, but
they all had tender spots about 'em somewheres,
and he had to shove 'em aside. So at last he was
about in despair. Then the St Louis papers begun
to talk a good deal about the balloon that was
going to sail to Europe, and Tom sort of thought
he wanted to go down and see what it looked
like, but couldn't make up his mind. But the papers went on talking, and so he allowed that
maybe if he didn't go he mightn't ever have another chance to see a balloon; and next, he found
out that Nat Parsons was going down to see it,
and that decided him, of course. He wasn't going to have Nat Parsons coming back bragging
about seeing the balloon, and him having to lis-

ten to it and keep quiet. So he wanted me and Jim to go too, and we went.

It was a noble big balloon, and had wings and fans and all sorts of things, and wasn't like any balloon you see in pictures. It was away out toward the edge of town, in a vacant lot, corner of Twelfth Street; and there was a big crowd around it, making fun of it, and making fun of the man—a lean pale feller with that soft kind of moonlight in his eyes, you know—and they kept saying it wouldn't go. It made him hot to hear them, and he would turn on them and shake his fist and say they was animals and blind, but some day they would find they had stood face to face with one of the men that lifts up nations and makes civilizations, and was too dull to know it; and right here on this spot their own children and grandchildren would build a monument to him that would outlast a thousand years, but his name would outlast the monument. And then the crowd would burst out in a laugh again, and yell at him, and ask him what was his name before he was married, and what he would take to not do it, and what was his sister's cat's grandmother's name, and all the things that a crowd says when they've got hold of a feller that they see they can plague. Well, some things they said was funny—yes, and mighty witty too, I ain't denying that—but all the same it warn't fair nor brave, all them people pitching on one, and they so glib and sharp, and him without any gift of talk to answer back with. But, good land! What did he want to sass back for? You see, it couldn't do him no good, and it was just nuts for them. They had him, you know. But that was his way. I reckon he couldn't help it; he was made so, I judge. He was a good enough sort of cretur, and hadn't no harm in him, and was just a genius, as the papers said, which wasn't his fault. We can't all be sound: we've got to be the way we're made. As near as I can make out, geniuses think they know it all, and so they won't take people's advice, but always go their own way, which makes everybody forsake them and despise them, and that is perfectly natural. If they was humbler, and listened and tried to learn, it would be better for them.

The part the professor was in was like a boat, and was big and roomy, and had watertight lockers around the inside to keep all sorts of things in, and a body could sit on them, and make beds on them, too. We went aboard, and there was twenty people there, snooping around and examining, and old Nat Parsons was there, too. The professor kept fussing around getting ready, and the people went ashore, drifting out one at a time, and old Nat he was the last. Of course it wouldn't do to let him go out behind us. We mustn't budge till he was gone, so we could be last ourselves.

But he was gone now, so it was time for us to follow. I heard a big shout, and turned around— the city was dropping from under us like a shot! It made me sick all through, I was so scared. Jim turned grey and couldn't say a word, and Tom didn't say nothing, but looked excited. The city went on dropping down, and down, and down; but we didn't seem to be doing nothing but just hang in the air and stand still. The houses got smaller and smaller, and the city pulled itself together, closer and closer, and the men and wagons got to looking like ants and bugs crawling around, and the streets like threads and cracks; and then it all kind of melted together, and there wasn't any city any more: it was only a big scar on the earth, and it seemed to me a body could see up the river and down the river about a thousand miles, though of course it wasn't so much. By and by the earth was a ball—just a round ball, of a dull colour, with shiny stripes wriggling and winding around over it, which was rivers. The Widder Douglas always told me the earth was round like a ball, but I never took any stock in a lot of them superstitions o' hers, and of course I paid no attention to that one, because I could see myself that the world was the shape of a plate, and flat. I used to go up on the hill, and take a look around and prove it for myself, because I reckon the best way to get a sure thing on a fact is to go and examine for yourself, and not take anybody's say-so. But I had to give in now that the widder was right. That is, she was right as to the rest of the world, but she warn't right about the part our village is in; that part is the shape of a plate, and flat, I take my oath!

The professor had been quiet all this time, as if he was asleep; but he broke loose now, and he was mighty bitter. He says something like this:

"Idiots! They said it wouldn't go; and they wanted to examine it, and spy around and get the

secret of it out of me. But I beat them. Nobody
knows the secret but me. Nobody knows what
makes it move but me; and it's a new power—a
new power, and a thousand times the strongest
in the earth! Steam's foolishness to it! They said
I couldn't go to Europe. To Europe! Why,
there's power aboard to last five years, and feed
for three months. They are fools! What do they
know about it? Yes, and they said my airship
was flimsy. Why, she's good for fifty years! I can
sail the skies all my life if I want to, and steer
where I please, though they laughed at that, and
said I couldn't. Couldn't steer! Come here, boy;
we'll see. You press these buttons as I tell you."

He made Tom steer the ship all about and
every which way, and learnt him the whole thing
in nearly no time; and Tom said it was perfectly
easy. He made him fetch the ship down 'most to
the earth, and had him spin her along so close to
the Illinois prairies that a body could talk to the
farmers, and hear everything they said perfectly
plain; and he flung out printed bills to them that
told about the balloon, and said it was going to
Europe. Tom got so he could steer straight for a
tree till he got nearly to it, and then dart up and

skin right along over the top of it. Yes, and he showed Tom how to land her; and he done it first-rate, too, and set her down in the prairies as soft as wool. But the minute we started to skip out the professor says, "No, you don't!" and shot her up in the air again. It was awful. I begun to beg and so did Jim; but it only give his temper a rise, and he begun to rage around and look wild out of his eyes, and I was scared of him.

Well, then he got on to his troubles again, and mourned and grumbled about the way he was treated, and couldn't seem to git over it, and especially people's saying his ship was flimsy. He scoffed at that, and at their saying she warn't simple and would be always getting out of order. Get out of order! That gravelled him; he said that she couldn't any more get out of order than the solar sister.

He got worse and worse, and I never see a person take on so. It give me the cold shivers to see him, and so it did Jim. By and by he got to yelling and screaming, and then he swore the world shouldn't ever have his secret at all now, it had treated him so mean. He said he would sail his balloon around the globe just to show what he could do, and then he would sink it in the sea, and sink us all along with it, too. Well, it was the awfulest fix to be in, and here was night coming on!

He give us something to eat, and made us go to the other end of the boat, and he laid down on a locker, where he could boss all the works, and put his old pepperbox revolver under his head, and said if anybody come fooling around there trying to land her, he would kill him.

We set scrunched up together, and thought considerable, but didn't say much—only just a word once in a while when a body had to say something or bust, we was so scared and worried. The night dragged along slow and lonesome. We was pretty low down, and the moonshine made everything soft and pretty, and the farmhouses looked snug and homeful, and we could hear the farm sounds, and wished we could be down there; but laws! We just slipped along over them like a ghost, and never left a track.

Away in the night, when all the sounds was late sounds, and the air had a late feel, and a late smell, too—about a two-o'clock feel, as near as

I could make out—Tom said the professor was so quiet this time he must be asleep, and we'd better –

"Better what?" I says in a whisper, and feeling sick all over, because I knowed what he was thinking about.

"Better slip back there and tie him, and land the ship," he says.

I says, "No, sir! Don't you budge, Tom Sawyer."

And Jim—well, Jim was kind o'gasping, he was so scared. He says:

"Oh, Mars Tom, don't! Ef you teches him, we's gone—we's gone sho'! I ain't gwine a-near him, not for nothin' in dis worl'. Mars Tom, he's plumb crazy."

Tom whispers and says, "That's why we've got to do something. If he wasn't crazy I wouldn't give shucks to be anywhere but here; you couldn't hire me to get out—now that I've got used to this balloon and over the scare of being cut loose from solid ground—if he was in his right mind. But it's no good politics, sailing around like this with a person that's out of his head, and says he's going round the world and then drown us all. We've got to do something, I tell you, and do it before he wakes up, too, or we mayn't ever get another chance. Come!"

But it made us turn cold and creepy just to think of it, and we said we wouldn't budge. So Tom was for slipping back there by himself to see if he couldn't get at the steering gear and land the ship. We begged and begged him not to, but it warn't no use; so he got down on his hands and knees, and begun to crawl an inch at a time, we a-holding our breath and watching. After he got to the middle of the boat he crept slower than ever, and it did seem like years to me. But at last we see him get to the professor's head, and sort of raise up soft and look a good spell in his face and listen. Then we see him begin to inch along again toward the professor's feet where the steering buttons was. Well, he got there all safe, and was reaching slow and steady toward the buttons, but he knocked down something that made a noise, and we see him slump down flat an' soft in the bottom, and lay still. The professor stirred, and says, "What's that?" But everybody kept dead still and quiet, and he begun to mutter and mumble and nestle, like a person that's going to wake up, and I thought I was going to die, I was so worried and scared.

Then a cloud slid over the moon, and I 'most cried, I was so glad. She buried herself deeper and deeper into the cloud, and it got so dark we couldn't see Tom. Then it began to sprinkle rain, and we could hear the professor fussing at his ropes and things and abusing the weather. We was afraid every minute he would touch Tom, and then we would be goners, and no help; but Tom, was already on his way back, and when we felt his hands on our knees my breath stopped sudden, and my heart fell down 'mongst my other works, because I couldn't tell in the dark but it might be the professor, which I thought it was.

Dear! I was so glad to have him back that I was just as near happy as a person could be that was up in the air that way with a deranged man. You can't land a balloon in the dark, and so I hoped it would keep on raining, for I didn't want Tom to go meddling any more and make us so awful uncomfortable. Well, I got my wish. It drizzled along the rest of the night, which wasn't long, though it did seem so; and at daybreak it cleared, and the world looked mighty soft and grey and pretty, and the forests and fields so good to see again, and the horses and cattle standing sober and thinking. Next, the sun come a-blazing up gay and splendid, and then we began to feel rusty and stretchy, and first we knowed we was all asleep.

3

Tom Explains

We went to sleep about four o'clock, and woke up about eight. The professor was setting back there at his end, looking glum. He pitched us some breakfast, but he told us not to come abaft the midship compass. That was about the middle of the boat. Well, when you are sharp-set, and you eat and satisfy yourself, everything looks pretty different from what it done before. It makes a body feel pretty near comfortable, even when he is up in a balloon with a genius. We got to talking together.

There was one thing that kept bothering me, and by and by I says:

"Tom, didn't we start east?"

"Yes."

"How fast have we been going?"

"Well, you heard what the professor said when he was raging round. Sometimes, he said, we was making fifty miles an hour, sometimes ninety, sometimes a hundred; said that with a gale to help he could make three hundred any time, and said if he wanted the gale, and wanted it blowing the right direction, he only had to go up higher or down lower to find it."

"Well, then, it's just as I reckoned. The professor lied."

"Why?"

"Because if we was going so fast we ought to be past Illinois, oughtn't we?"

"Certainly."

"Well, we ain't."

"What's the reason we ain't?"

"I know by the colour. We're right over Illinois yet. And you can see for yourself that Indiana ain't in sight."

"I wonder what's the matter with you, Huck. You know by the colour?"

"Yes, of course I do."

"What's the colour got to do with it?"

"It's got everything to do with it. Illinois is

green, Indiana is pink. You show me any pink down here, if you can. No, sir; it's green."

"Indiana pink? Why, what a lie!"

"It ain't no lie; I've seen it on the map, and it's pink."

You never see a person so aggravated and disgusted. He says:

"Well, if I was such a numskull as you, Huck Finn, I would jump over. Seen it on the map! Huck Finn, did you reckon the states was the same colour out-of-doors as they are on the map?"

"Tom Sawyer, what's a map for? Ain't it to learn you facts?"

"Of course."

"Well, then, how's it going to do that if it tells lies? That's what I want to know."

"Shucks, you muggins! It don't tell lies."

"It don't, don't it?"

"No, it don't."

"All right, then; if it don't, there ain't no two states the same colour. You git around that, if you can, Tom Sawyer."

He see I had him, and Jim see it too; and I tell you, I felt pretty good, for Tom Sawyer was al-

ways a hard person to get ahead of. Jim slapped
his leg and says:

"I tell you! Dat's smart, dat's right down
smart. Ain't no use, Mars Tom; he got you dis
time, sho'!" He slapped his leg again, and says,
"My lan', but it was a smart one!"

I never felt so good in my life; and yet I didn't
know I was saying anything much till it was out.
I was just mooning along, perfectly careless, and
not expecting anything was going to happen,
and never thinking of such a thing at all, when,
all of a sudden, out it came. Why, it was just as
much a surprise to me as it was to any of them. It
was just the same way it is when a person is
munching along on a hunk of corn pone, and not
thinking about anything, and all of a sudden
bites into a di'mond. Now all that he knows first
off is that it's some kind of gravel he's bit into;
but he don't find out it's a di'mond till he gits it
out and brushes off the sand and crumbs and one
thing or another, and has a look at it, and then
he's surprised and glad—yes, and proud too;
though when you come to look the thing straight
in the eye, he ain't entitled to as much credit as
he would 'a' been if he'd been hunting

di'monds. You can see the difference easy if you
think it over. You see, an accident, that way,
ain't fairly as big a thing as a thing that's done a-
purpose. Anybody could find that di'mond in
that corn pone; but mind you, it's got to be
somebody that's got that kind of a corn pone.
That's where that feller's credit comes in, you
see; and that's where mine comes in. I don't
claim no great things—I don't reckon I could 'a'
done it again—but I done it that time; that's all I
claim. And I hadn't no more idea I could do such
a thing, and warn't any more thinking about it or
trying to, than you be this minute. Why, I was
just as ca'm, a body couldn't be any ca'mer, and
yet, all of a sudden, out it come. I've often
thought of that time, and I can remember just the
way everything looked, same as if it was only
last week. I can see it all: beautiful rolling country with woods and fields and lakes for hundreds
and hundreds of miles all around, and towns and
villages scattered everywheres under us, here
and there and yonder; and the professor mooning over a chart on his little table, and Tom's cap
flopping in the rigging where it was hung up to
dry. And one thing in particular was a bird right

alongside, not ten foot off, going our way and trying to keep up, but losing ground all the time; and a railroad train doing the same thing down there, sliding among the trees and farms, and pouring out a long cloud of black smoke and now and then a little puff of white; and when the white was gone so long you had almost forgot it, you would hear a little faint toot, and that was the whistle. And we left the bird and the train both behind, 'way behind, and done it easy, too.

But Tom he was huffy, and said me and Jim was a couple of ignorant blatherskites, and then he says:

"Suppose there's a brown calf and a big brown dog, and an artist is making a picture of them. What is the main thing that that artist has got to do? He has got to paint them so you can tell them apart the minute you look at them, hain't he? Of course. Well, then, do you want him to go and paint both of them brown? Certainly you don't. He paints one of them blue, and then you can't make no mistake. It's just the same with the maps. That's why they make every state a different colour; it ain't to deceive you, it's to keep you from deceiving yourself."

But I couldn't see no argument about that, and neither could Jim. Jim shook his head, and says:

"Why, Mars Tom, if you knowed what chuckleheads dem painters is, you'd wait a long time before you'd fetch one er dem in to back up a fac'. I's gwine to tell you, den you kin see for you'self. I see one of 'em a-paintin' away, one day, down in ole Hank Wilson's back lot, en I went down to see, en he was paintin' dat old bridle cow wid de near horn gone—you knows de one I means. En I ask him what he's paintin' her for, en he say when he git her painted, de picture's wuth a hundred dollars. Mars Tom, he could 'a' got de cow fer fifteen, en I tole him so. Well, sah, if you'll b'lieve me, he jes' shuck his head, dat painter did, en went on a-dobbin'. Bless you, Mars Tom, dey don't know nothin'."

Tom lost his temper. I notice a person 'most always does that's got laid out in an argument. He told us to shut up, and maybe we'd feel better. Then he see a town clock away off down yonder, and he took up the glass and looked at it, and then looked at his silver turnip, and then at the clock, and then at the turnip again, and says:

"That's funny! That clock's near about an hour fast."

So he put up his turnip. Then he see another clock, and took a look, and it was an hour fast too. That puzzled him.

"That's a mighty curious thing," he says. "I don't understand it."

Then he took the glass and hunted up another clock, and sure enough it was an hour fast too. Then his eyes began to spread and his breath to come out kinder gaspy like, and he says:

"Ger-reat Scott, it's the longitude!"

I says, considerably scared:

"Well, what's been and gone and happened now?"

"Why, the thing that's happened is that this old bladder has slid over Illinois and Indiana and Ohio like nothing, and this is the east end of Pennsylvania or New York, or somewheres around there."

"Tom Sawyer, you don't mean it!"

"Yes, I do, and it's dead sure. We've covered about fifteen degrees of longitude since we left St Louis yesterday afternoon, and them clocks are right. We've come close on to eight hundred miles."

I didn't believe it, but it made the cold streaks trickle down my back just the same. In my experience I knowed it wouldn't take much short of two weeks to do it down the Mississippi on a raft.

Jim was working his mind and studying. Pretty soon he says:

"Mars Tom, did you say dem clocks uz right?"

"Yes, they're right."

"Ain't yo watch right, too?"

"She's right for St Louis, but she's an hour wrong for here."

"Mars Tom, is you tryin' to let on dat de time ain't de same everywheres?"

"No, it ain't the same everywheres, by a long shot."

Jim looked distressed, and says:

"It grieves me to hear you talk like dat, Mars Tom; I's right down ashamed to hear you talk like dat, arter de way you's been raised. Yassir, it'd break yo' aunt Polly's heart to hear you."

Tom was astonished. He looked Jim over wondering, and didn't say nothing, and Jim went on:

"Mars Tom, who put de people out yonder in

St Louis? De Lord done it. Who put de people here whar we is? De Lord done it. Ain' dey bofe his children? 'Cose dey is. Well, den! is he gwine to scriminate 'twixt 'em?"

"Scriminate! I never heard such ignorance. There ain't no discriminating about it. When he makes you and some more of his children black, and makes the rest of us white, what do you call that?"

Jim could see the p'int. He was stuck. He couldn't answer. Tom says:

"He does discriminate, you see, when he wants to; but this case here ain't no discrimination of his, it's man's. The Lord made the day, and he made the night; but he didn't invent the hours, and he didn't distribute them around. Man did that."

"Mars Tom, is dat so? Man done it?"

"Certainly."

"Who tole him he could?"

"Nobody. He never asked."

Jim studied a minute, and says:

"Well, dat do beat me. I wouldn't 'a' tuck no such resk. But some people ain't scared o' nothin'. Dey bangs right ahead; dey don't care what happens. So den dey's allays an hour's diff'unce everywhah, Mars Tom?"

"An hour? No! It's four minutes different for every degree of longitude, you know. Fifteen of 'em's an hour, thirty of 'em's two hours, and so on. When it's one o'clock Tuesday morning in England, it's eight o'clock the night before in New York."

Jim moved a little way along the locker, and you could see he was insulted. He kept shaking his head and muttering, and so I slid along to him and patted him on the leg, and petted him up, and got him over the worst of his feelings, and then he says:

"Mars Tom talkin' sich talk as dat! Choosday in one place en Monday in t'other, bofe in the same day! Huck, dis ain't no place to joke—up here whah we is. Two days in one day! How you gwine to get two days inter one day? Can't git two hours inter one hour, kin you? Can't git two men inter one man's skin, kin you? Can't git two gallons of whisky inter a one-gallon jug, kin you? No, sir, 'twould strain the jug. Yes, en even den you couldn't, I don't believe. Why, looky here, Huck, s'posen de Choosday was New

Year's—now den! is you gwine to tell me it's dis year in one place en las' year in t'other, bofe in de identical same minute? It's de beatenest rubbage! I can't stan' it—I can't stan' to hear tell 'bout it." Then he begun to shiver and turn grey, and Tom says:

"Now what's the matter? What's the trouble?"

Jim could hardly speak, but he says:

"Mars Tom, you ain't jokin', en it's so?"

"No, I'm not, and it is so."

Jim shivered again, and says:

"Den dat Monday could be de las' day, en dey wouldn't be no las' day in England, en de dead wouldn't be called. We mustn't go over dah, Mars Tom. Please git him to turn back; I wants to be whah—"

All of a sudden we see something, and all jumped up, and forgot everything and begun to gaze. Tom says:

"Ain't that the—" He catched his breath, then says; "It is, sure as you live! It's the ocean!"

That made me and Jim catch our breath, too. Then we all stood petrified but happy, for none of us had ever seen an ocean, or ever expected to. Tom kept muttering:

st the talk ran dry altogether, and
re and "thunk," as Jim calls it, and
vord the longest time.

sor never stirred till the sun was
en he stood up and put a kind of tri-
eye, and Tom said it was a sextant
s taking the sun to see whereabouts
n was. Then he ciphered a little and
a book, and then he begun to carry on
e said lots of wild things, and, among
e said he would keep up this hundred-
t till the middle of tomorrow afternoon,
n he'd land in London.

aid we would be humbly thankful.

vas turning away, but he whirled around
we said that, and give us a long look of his
est kind—one of the maliciousest and
iciousest looks I ever see. Then he says:

ou want to leave me. Don't try to deny it."

e didn't know what to say, so we held in and
n't say nothing at all.

He went aft and set down, but he couldn't
em to git that thing out of his mind. Every now
nd then he would rip out something about it,
and try to make us answer him, but we dasn't.

"Atlantic Ocean—Atlantic. Land, don't it sound great! And that's it—and we are looking at it—we! Why, it's just too splendid to believe!"

Then we see a big bank of black smoke; and when we got nearer, it was a city—and a monster she was, too, with a thick fringe of ships around one edge; and we wondered if it was New York, and begun to jaw and dispute about it, and, first we knowed, it slid from under us and went flying behind, and here we was, out over the very ocean itself, and going like a cyclone. Then we woke up, I tell you!

We made a break aft and raised a wail, and begun to beg the professor to turn back and land us, but he jerked out his pistol and motioned us back, and we went, but nobody will ever know how bad we felt.

The land was gone, all but a little streak, like a snake, away off on the edge of the water, and down under us was just ocean, ocean, ocean—millions of miles of it, heaving and pitching and squirming, and white sprays blowing from the wave tops, and only a few ships in sight, wallowing around and laying over, first on one side and then on t'other, and sticking their bows under and then their sterns; and before long there warn't no ships at all, and we had the sky and the whole ocean to ourselves, and the roomiest place I ever see and the lonesomest.

And it got lonesom

the big sky up there,

the ocean down there

just the waves. All arou

the sky and the water cor

strous big ring it was, and

centre of it—plumb in the c

along like a prairie fire, bu

difference, we couldn't seem

tre no way. I couldn't see that

inch on that ring. It made a boc

was so curious and unaccountabl

Well, everything was so awful st

to talking in a very low voice, and

ting creepier and lonesomer and le

4

Storm

And it got lonesomer and lonesomer. There was the big sky up there, empty and awful deep; and the ocean down there without a thing on it but just the waves. All around us was a ring, where the sky and the water come together; yes, a monstrous big ring it was, and we right in the dead centre of it—plumb in the centre. We was racing along like a prairie fire, but it never made any difference, we couldn't seem to git past that centre no way. I couldn't see that we ever gained an inch on that ring. It made a body feel creepy, it was so curious and unaccountable.

Well, everything was so awful still that we got to talking in a very low voice, and kept on getting creepier and lonesomer and less and less talky, till at last the talk ran dry altogether, and we just set there and "thunk," as Jim calls it, and never said a word the longest time.

The professor never stirred till the sun was overhead; then he stood up and put a kind of triangle to his eye, and Tom said it was a sextant and he was taking the sun to see whereabouts the balloon was. Then he ciphered a little and looked in a book, and then he begun to carry on again. He said lots of wild things, and, among others, he said he would keep up this hundred-mile gait till the middle of tomorrow afternoon, and then he'd land in London.

We said we would be humbly thankful.

He was turning away, but he whirled around when we said that, and give us a long look of his blackest kind—one of the maliciousest and suspiciousest looks I ever see. Then he says:

"You want to leave me. Don't try to deny it."

We didn't know what to say, so we held in and didn't say nothing at all.

He went aft and set down, but he couldn't seem to git that thing out of his mind. Every now and then he would rip out something about it, and try to make us answer him, but we dasn't.

It got lonesomer and lonesomer right along, and it did seem to me I couldn't stand it. It was still worse when night begun to come on. By and by Tom pinched me and whispers:

"Look!"

I took a glance aft, and see the professor taking a whet out of a bottle. I didn't like the looks of that. By and by he took another drink, and pretty soon he begun to sing. It was dark now, and getting black and stormy. He went on singing, wilder and wilder, and the thunder begun to mutter, and the wind to wheeze and moan among the ropes, and altogether it was awful. It got so black we couldn't see him any more, and wished we couldn't hear him, but we could. Then he got still; but he warn't still ten minutes till we got suspicious, and wished he would start up his noise again, so we could tell where he was. By and by there was a flash of lightning, and we see him start to get up, but he staggered and fell down. We heard him scream out in the dark:

"They don't want to go to England. All right, I'll change the course. They want to leave me. I know they do. Well, they shall—and now!"

I 'most died when he said that. Then he was still again—still so long I couldn't bear it, and it did seem to me the lightning wouldn't ever come again. But at last there was a blessed flash, and there he was, on his hands and knees crawling, and not four feet from us. My, but his eyes was terrible! He made a lunge for Tom, and says, "Overboard you go!" but it was already pitch dark again, and I couldn't see whether he got him or not, and Tom didn't make a sound.

There was another long, horrible wait; then there was a flash, and I see Tom's head sink down outside the boat and disappear. He was on the rope ladder that dangled down in the air from the gunnel. The professor let off a shout and jumped for him, and straight off it was pitch dark again, and Jim groaned out, "Po' Mars Tom, he's a goner!" and made a jump for the professor, but the professor warn't there.

Then we heard a couple of terrible screams, and then another not so loud, and then another that was 'way below, and you could only just hear it; and I heard Jim say, "Po' Mars Tom!"

Then it was awful still, and I reckon a person could 'a' counted four thousand before the next flash come. When it come I see Jim on his knees, with his arms on the locker and his face buried in them, and he was crying. Before I could look over the edge it was dark again, and I was glad, because I didn't want to see. But when the next flash come, I was watching, and down there I see somebody a-swinging in the wind on the ladder, and it was Tom!

"Come up!" I shouts; "come up, Tom!"

His voice was so weak, and the wind roared so, I couldn't make out what he said, but I thought he asked was the professor up there. I shouts:

"No, he's down in the ocean! Come up! Can we help you?"

Of course, all this in the dark.

"Huck, who is you hollerin' at?"

"I'm hollerin' at Tom."

"Oh, Huck, how kin you act so, when you know po' Mars Tom—" Then he let off an awful scream, and flung his head and his arms back and let off another one, because there was a white glare just then, and he had raised up his face just in time to see Tom's, as white as snow, rise above the gunnel and look him right in the eye. He thought it was Tom's ghost, you see.

Tom clumb aboard, and when Jim found it was him, and not his ghost, he hugged him, and called him all sorts of loving names, and carried on like he was gone crazy, he was so glad. Says I:

"What did you wait for, Tom? Why didn't you come up at first?"

"I dasn't, Huck. I knowed somebody plunged down past me, but I didn't know who it was in the dark. It could 'a' been you, it could 'a' been Jim."

That was the way with Tom Sawyer—always sound. He warn't coming up till he knowed where the professor was.

The storm let go about this time with all its might; and it was dreadful the way the thunder boomed and tore, and the lightning glared out, and the wind sung and screamed in the rigging, and the rain come down. One second you couldn't see your hand before you, and the next you could count the threads in your coat sleeve, and see a whole wide desert of waves pitching and tossing through a kind of veil of rain. A storm like that is the loveliest thing there is, but it ain't at its best when you are up in the sky and lost, and it's wet and lonesome, and there's just been a death in the family.

We set there huddled up in the bow, and talked low about the poor professor; and everybody was sorry for him, and sorry the world had made fun of him, and treated him so harsh, when he was doing the best he could, and hadn't a friend nor nobody to encourage him and keep him from brooding his mind away and going deranged. There was plenty of clothes and blankets and everything at the other end, but we thought we'd ruther take the rain than go meddling back there.

5

Tom Respects the Flea

"Noon!" says Tom, and so it was. His shadder was just a blot around his feet. We looked, and the Grinnage clock was so close to twelve the difference didn't amount to nothing. So Tom said London was right north of us or right south of us, one or t'other, and he reckoned by the weather and the sand and the camels it was north; and a good many miles north, too; as many as from New York to the city of Mexico, he guessed.

Jim said he reckoned a balloon was a good deal the fastest thing in the world, unless it might be some kinds of birds—a wild pigeon, maybe, or a railroad.

But Tom said he had read about railroads in England going nearly a hundred miles an hour for a little ways, and there never was a bird in the world that could do that—except one, and that was a flea.

"A flea? Why, Mars Tom, in de fust place he ain't a bird strickly speakin' –"

"He ain't a bird, eh? Well, then, what is he?"

"I don't rightly know, Mars Tom, but I speck he's only jist a' animal. No, I reckon dat won't do, nuther, he ain't big enough for a' animal. He mus' be a bug. Yassir, dat's what he is, he's a bug."

"I bet he ain't, but let it go. What's your second place?"

"Well, in de second place, birds is creturs dat goes a long ways, but a flea don't."

"He don't, don't he? Come, now, what is a long distance, if you know?"

"Why, it's miles, and lot of 'em—anybody knows dat."

"Can't a man walk miles?"

"Yassir, he kin."

"As many as a railroad?"

"Yassir, if you gave him time."

"Can't a flea?"

"Well—I s'pose so—ef you gives him heaps of time."

"Now you begin to see, don't you, that distance ain't the thing to judge by, at all; it's the time it takes to go the distance in that counts, ain't it?"

"Well, hit do look sorter so, but I wouldn't 'a' b'lieved it, Mars Tom."

"It's a matter of proportion, that's what it is; and when you come to gauge a thing's speed by its size, where's your bird and your railroad 'longside of a flea? The fastest man can't run more than about ten miles in an hour—not much over ten thousand times his own length. But all the books says any common ordinary third-class flea can jump a hundred and fifty times his own length; yes, and he can make five jumps a second too—seven hundred and fifty times his own length, in one little second—for he don't fool away time stopping and starting—he does them both at the same time; you'll see, if you try to put your finger on him. Now that's a common, ordinary, third-class flea's gait; but you take an Eyetalian first-class, that's been the pet of nobility all his life, and hasn't ever knowed what want or sickness or exposure was, and he can jump more than three hundred times his own length, and keep it up all day, five such jumps every second, which is fifteen hundred times his own length. Well, suppose a man could go fifteen hundred times his own length in a second— say, a mile and a half. It's ninety miles a minute; it's considerable more than five thousand miles an hour. Where's your man now?—yes, and your bird, and your railroad, and your balloon? Laws, they don't amount to shucks 'longside of a flea. A flea is just a comet b'iled down small."

Jim was a good deal astonished, and so was I. Jim said:

"Is dem figgers jist edjackly true, en no jokin' en no lies, Mars Tom?"

"Yes, they are; they're perfectly true."

"Well, den, honey, a body's got to respec' a flea. I ain't had no respec' for um befo', sca'sely, but dey ain't no gittin' roun' it, dey do deserve it, dat's certain."

"Well, I bet they do. They've got ever so much more sense, and brains, and brightness, in proportion to their size, than any other cretur in the world. A person can learn them 'most anything; and they learn it quicker than any other cretur, too. They've been learnt to haul little carriages in harness, and go this way and that way and t'other way according to their orders; yes, and to march and drill like soldiers, doing it as exact, according to orders, as soldiers does it. They've been learnt to do all sorts of hard and trouble-some things. S'pose you could cultivate a flea up to the size of a man, and keep his natural smart-ness a-growing and a-growing right along up, bigger and bigger, and keener and keener, in the same proportion—where'd the human race be, do you reckon? That flea would be President of the United States, and you couldn't any more prevent it than you can prevent lightning."

"My lan', Mars Tom, I never knowed dey was so much to de beas'. No, sir, I never had no idea of it, and dat's de fac'."

"There's more to him, by a long sight, then there is to any other cretur, man or beast, in pro-portion to size. He's the interestingest of them all. People have so much to say about an ant's strength, and an elephant's, and a locomotive's. Shucks, they don't begin with a flea. He can lift two or three hundred times his own weight. And none of them can come anywhere near it. And, moreover, he has got notions of his own, and is very particular, and you can't fool him; his instinct, or his judgement, or whatever it is, is perfectly sound and clear, and don't ever make a mistake. People think all humans are alike to a flea. It ain't so. There's folks that he won't go near, hungry or not hungry, and I'm one of them. I've never had one of them on me in my life."

"Mars Tom!"

"It's so; I ain't joking."

"Well, sah, I hain't ever heard de likes o' dat befo'."

Jim couldn't believe it, and I couldn't; so we had to drop down to the sand and git a supply and see. Tom was right. They went for me and Jim by the thousand, but not one of them lit on Tom. There warn't no explaining it, but there it was and there warn't no getting around it. He said it had always been just so, and he'd just as soon be where there was a million of them as not; they'd never touch him nor bother him.

We went up to the cold weather to freeze 'em out, and stayed a little spell, and then came back

to the comfortable weather and went lazying
along twenty or twenty-five miles an hour, the
way we'd been doing for the last few hours. The
reason was, that the longer we was in that solemn, peaceful desert, the more the hurry and
fuss got kind of soothed down in us, and the
more happier and contented and satisfied we got
to feeling, and the more we got to liking the
desert, and then loving it. So we had cramped
the speed down, as I was saying, and was having
a most noble good lazy time, sometimes watching through the glasses, sometimes stretched out
on the lockers reading, sometimes taking a nap.

It didn't seem like we was the same lot that
was in such a state to find land and git ashore,
but it was. But we had got over that—clean over
it. We was used to the balloon now and not
afraid any more, and didn't want to be
anywheres else. Why, it seemed just like home;
it 'most seemed as if I had been born and raised
in it, and Jim and Tom said the same. And always I had had hateful people around me, a-nag-
ging at me, and pestering of me, and scolding,
and finding fault, and fussing and bothering, and
sticking to me, and keeping after me, and mak-

ing me do this, and making me do that and t'other, and always selecting out the things I didn't want to do, and then giving me Sam Hill because I shirked and done something else, and just aggravating the life out of a body all the time; but up here in the sky it was so still and sunshiny and lovely, and plenty to eat, and plenty of sleep, and strange things to see, and no nagging and no pestering, and no good people, and just holiday all the time. Land, I warn't in no hurry to git out and buck at civilization again. Now, one of the worst things about civilization is, that anybody that gits a letter with trouble in it comes and tells you all about it and makes you feel bad, and the newspapers fetches you the troubles of everybody all over the world, and keeps you downhearted and dismal 'most all the time, and it's such a heavy load for a person. I hate them newspapers; and I hate letters; and if I had my way I wouldn't allow nobody to load his troubles onto other folks he ain't acquainted with, on t'other side of the world, that way. Well, up in a balloon there ain't any of that, and it's the darlingest place there is.

We had supper, and that night was one of the

prettiest nights I ever see. The moon made it just like daylight, only a heap softer; and once we see a lion standing all alone by himself, just all alone on the earth, it seemed like, and his shadder laid on the sand by him like a puddle of ink. That's the kind of moonlight to have.

Mainly we laid on our backs and talked; we didn't want to go to sleep. Tom said we was right in the midst of the Arabian Nights now. He said it was right along here that one of the cutest things in that book happened; so we looked down and watched while he told about it, because there ain't anything that is so interesting to look at as a place that a book has talked about. It was a tale about a camel driver that had lost his camel, and he came along the desert and met a man, and says:

"Have you run across a stray camel today?"

And the man says:

"Was he blind in his left eye?"

"Yes."

"Had he lost an upper front tooth?"

"Yes."

"Was his off-hind leg lame?"

"Yes."

"Was he loaded with millet seed on one side and honey on the other?"

"Yes, but you needn't go into no more details—that's the one, and I'm in a hurry. Where did you see him?"

"I hain't seen him at all," the man says.

"Hain't seen him at all? How can you describe him so close, then?"

"Because when a person knows how to use his eyes, everything has got a meaning to it; but most people's eyes ain't any good to them. I know he was lame in his off-hind leg because he had favoured that foot and trod light on it, and his track showed it. I knowed he was blind in his left side because he only nibbled grass on the right side of the trail. I knowed he had lost an upper front tooth because where he bit into the sod his teeth print showed it. The millet seed sifted out on one side—the ants told me that; the honey leaked all about your camel, but I hain't seen him."

Jim says:

"Go on, Mars Tom, hit's a mighty good tale, and powerful interestin'."

"That's all," Tom says.

"All?" says Jim, astonished. "What 'come o' de camel?"

"I don't know."

"Mars Tom, don't de tale say?"

"No."

Jim puzzled a minute, then he says:

"Well! Ef dat ain't de beatenes' tale ever I struck. Jist gits to the place whah de intrust is gittin' red-hot, en down she breaks. Why, Mars Tom, dey ain't no sense in a tale dat acts like dat. Hain't you got no idea whether de man got de camel back er not?"

"No I haven't."

I see myself there warn't no sense in the tale, to chop square off that way before it come to anything, but I warn't going to say so, because I could see Tom was souring up pretty fast over the way it flatted out and the way Jim had popped onto the weak place in it, and I don't think it's fair for everybody to pile into a feller when he's down. But Tom he whirls on me and says:

"What do you think of the tale?"

Of course, then, I had to come out and make a clean breast and say it did seem to me, too, same as it did to Jim, that as long as the tale stopped square in the middle and never got no place, it really warn't worth the trouble of telling.

Tom's chin dropped on his breast, and 'stead of being mad, as I reckoned he'd be, to hear me scoff at his tale that way, he seemed to be only sad; and he says:

"Some people can see, and some can't—just as the man said. Let alone a camel, if a cyclone had gone by, you duffers wouldn't 'a' noticed the tracks."

I don't know what he meant by that, and he didn't say; it was just one of his irrulevances, I reckon—he was full of them, sometimes, when he was in a close place and couldn't see no other way out—but I didn't mind. We'd spotted the soft place in that tale sharp enough, he couldn't git away from that little fact. It gravelled him like the nation, too, I reckon, much as he tried not to let on.

6

The Disappearing Lake

We had an early breakfast in the morning, and
set looking down on the desert, and the weather
was ever so bammy and lovely, although we
warn't high up. You have to come down lower
and lower after sundown in the desert, because it
cools off so fast; and so by the time it is getting
toward dawn, you are skimming along only a little ways above the sand.

We was watching the shadder of the balloon
slide along the ground, and now and then gazing
off across the desert to see if anything was stirring, and then down on the shadder again, when
all of a sudden almost right under us we see a lot
of men and camels laying scattered about, perfectly quiet, like they was asleep.

We shut off the power, and backed up and

stood over them, and then we see that they was
all dead. It give us the cold shivers. And it made
us hush down, too, and talk low, like people at a
funeral. We dropped down slow and stopped,
and me and Tom clumb down and went among
them. There was men, and women, and children.
They was dried by the sun, and dark and shriv-
elled and leathery, like the pictures of mummies
you see in books. And yet they looked just as
human, you wouldn't 'a' believed it; just like
they was asleep.

Some of the people and animals was partly
covered with sand, but most of them not, for the
sand was thin there, and the bed was gravel and
hard. Most of the clothes had rotted away; and
when you took hold of a rag, it tore with a touch,
like spider web. Tom reckoned they had been
there for years.

Some of the men had rusty guns by them,
some had swords on and had shawl belts with
long, silver-mounted pistols stuck in them. All
the camels had their loads on yet, but the packs
had busted or rotted and spilt the freight out on
the ground. We didn't reckon the swords was
any good to the dead people any more, so we

took one apiece, and some pistols. We took a small box, too, because it was so handsome and inlaid so fine; and then we wanted to bury the people; but there warn't no way to do it that we could think of, nothing to do it with but sand, and that would blow away again, of course.

Then we mounted high and sailed away, and pretty soon that black spot on the sand was out of sight, and we wouldn't ever see them poor people again in this world. We wondered, and reasoned, and tried to guess how they come to be there, and how it all happened to them, but we couldn't make it out. First we thought maybe they got lost, and wandered around and about till their food and water give out and they starved to death; but Tom said no wild animals nor vultures hadn't meddled with them, and so that guess wouldn't do. So at last we give it up, and judged we wouldn't think about it no more, because it made us low spirited.

Then we opened the box, and it had gems and jewels in it, quite a pile, and some little veils of the kind of dead women had on, with fringes made out of curious gold money that we warn't acquainted with. We wondered if we better go and try to find them again, and give it back; but Tom thought it over and said no, it was a country that was full of robbers, and they would come and steal it; and then the sin would be on us for putting the temptation in their way. So we went on; but I wished we had took all they had, so there wouldn't 'a' been no temptation at all left.

We had had two hours of that blazing weather down there, and was dreadful thirsty when we got aboard again. We went straight for the water, but it was spoiled and bitter, besides being pretty near hot enough to scald your mouth. We couldn't drink it. It was Mississippi River water, the best in the world, and we stirred up the mud in it to see if that would help, but no, the mud wasn't any better than the water.

Well, we hadn't been so very, very thirsty before, while we was interested in the lost people, but we was now, and as soon as we found we couldn't have a drink, we was more than thirty-five times as thirsty as we was a quarter of a minute before. Why, in a little while we wanted to hold our mouths open and pant like a dog.

Tom said to keep a sharp lookout, all around, everywheres, because we'd got to find an oasis or there warn't no telling what would happen. So we done it. We kept the glasses gliding around all the time, till our arms got so tired we couldn't hold them any more. Two hours—three hours—just gazing and gazing, and nothing but sand, sand, sand and you could see the quivering heat shimmer playing over it. Dear, dear, a body don't know what real misery is till he is thirsty all the way through and is certain he ain't ever going to come to any water any more. At last I couldn't stand it to look around on them baking plains; I laid down on the locker, and give it up.

But by and by Tom raised a whoop, and there she was! A lake, wide and shiny, with pa'm trees leaning over it asleep, and their shadders in the water just as soft and delicate as ever you see. I never see anything look so good. It was a long ways off, but that warn't anything to us; we just slapped on a hundred-mile gait, and calculated to be there in seven minutes; but she stayed the same old distance away, all the time; we couldn't seem to gain on her; yes, sir, just as far, and shiny, and like a dream; but we couldn't get no nearer; and at last, all of a sudden, she was gone!

Tom's eyes took a spread, and he says:

"Boys, it was a myridge!" Said it like he was glad. I didn't see nothing to be glad about. I says:

"Maybe. I don't care nothing about its name, the thing I want to know is, what's become of it?"

Jim was trembling all over, and so scared he couldn't speak, but he wanted to ask that question himself if he could 'a' done it. Tom says:

"What's become of it? Why, you see yourself it's gone."

He looked me over and says:

"Well, now, Huck Finn, where would it go to! Don't you know what a myridge is?"

"No, I don't. What is it?"

"It ain't anything but imagination. There ain't anything to it."

It warmed me up to hear him talk like that, and I says:

"What's the use you talking that kind of stuff, Tom Sawyer? Didn't I see the lake?"

"Yes—you think you did."

"I don't think nothing about it, I did see it."

"I tell you you didn't see it either—because it warn't there to see."

It astonished Jim to hear him talk so, and he broke in and says, kind of pleading and distressed:

"Mars Tom, please don't say sich things in sich an awful time as dis. You ain't only reskin' yo' own self, but you's reskin' us—same way like Anna Nias en Siffira. De lake wus dah—I seen it jis' as plain as I sees you en Huck dis minute."

I says:

"Why, he seen it himself! He was the very one that seen it first. Now, then!"

"Yes, Mars Tom, hit's so—you can't deny it. We all seen it, en dat prove it was dah."

"Proves it! How doed it prove it?"

"Some way it does in de courts en everywheres, Mars Tom. One pusson might be drunk, or dreamy, or suthin', en he could be mistaken; en two might, maybe; but I tell you, sah, when three sees a thing, drunk or sober, it's so. Dey ain't no gittin' aroun' dat, en you knows it, Mars Tom."

"I don't know nothing of the kind. There used to be forty thousand million people that seen the sun move from one side of the sky to the other every day. Did that prove that the sun done it?"

" 'Course it did. En besides, dey warn't no 'casion to prove it. A body 'at's got any sense ain't gwine to doubt it. Dah she is now—a-sailin' thoo de sky, like she allays done."

Tom turned on me, then, and says:

"What do you say—is the sun standing still?"

"Tom Sawyer, what's the use to ask such a jackass question? Anybody that ain't blind can see it don't stand still."

"Well," he said, "I'm lost in the sky with no company but a passel of lowdown animals that don't know more than the head boss of a university did three or four hundred years ago."

It warn't fair play, and I let him know it. I says:

"Throwin' mud ain't arguin', Tom Sawyer."

"Oh, my goodness, oh, my goodness gracious, dah's de lake ag'in!" yelled Jim, just then. "Now, Mars Tom, what you gwine to say?"

Yes, sir, there was the lake again, away yonder across the desert, perfectly plain, trees and all, just the same as it was before. I says:

"I reckon you're satisfied now, Tom Sawyer."

But he says, perfectly ca'm:

"Yes, satisfied there ain't no lake there."

Jim says:

"Don't talk so, Mars Tom—it sk'yers me to hear you. It's so hot, en you's so thirsty, dat you ain't in yo' right mine, Mars Tom. Oh, but don't she look good! I declah I doan' know how I's gwine to wait tell we gits dah, I's so thirsty."

"Well, you'll have to wait; and it won't do you no good either, because there ain't no lake there, I tell you."

I says:

"Jim, don't you take your eye off of it, and I won't either."

"'Deed I won't; en bless you, honey, I couldn't ef I wanted to."

We went a-tearing along toward it, piling the miles behind us like nothing, but never gaining an inch on it—and all of a sudden it was gone again! Jim staggered, and 'most fell down. When he got his breath he says, gasping like a fish:

"Mars Tom, hit's a ghos', dat's what it is, en I hopes to goodness we ain't gwine to see it no mo'. Dey's been a lake, en suthin's happened, en de lake's dead, en we's seen its ghos', we's seen it twise, en dat's proof. De desert's ha'nted, it's ha'nted, sho; oh, Mars Tom, let's git outen it; I'd ruther die den have de night ketch us in it ag'in en de ghos' er dat lake come a-mournin' aroun' us en we asleep en doan' know de danger we's in."

"Ghost, you gander! It ain't anything but air and heat and thirstiness pasted together by a person's imagination. If I—gimme the glass!"

He grabbed it and begun to gaze off to the right.

"It's a flock of birds," he says. "It's getting to-ward sundown, and they're making a beeline across our track for somewheres. They mean business—maybe they're going for food or water, or both. Let her go to starboard!—Port your hellum! Hard down! There—ease up—steady, as you go."

We shut down some of the power, so as not to out-speed them, and took out after them. We went skimming along a quarter of a mile behind them, and when we had followed them an hour and a half and was getting pretty discouraged, and was thirsty clean to unendurableness, Tom says:

"Take the glass, one of you, and see what that is, away ahead of the birds."

Jim got the first glimpse, and slumped down on on the locker sick. He was 'most crying, and says:

"She's dah ag'in, Mars Tom, she's dah ag'in, en I knows I's gwine to die, 'case when a body sees a ghos' de third time, dat's what it means. I wisht I'd never come in dis balloon, dat I does."

He wouldn't look no more, and what he said made me afraid, too, because I knowed it was true, for that has always been the way with ghosts; so then I wouldn't look any more, either. Both of us begged Tom to turn off and go some other way, but he wouldn't, and said we was ignorant superstitious blatherskites. Yes, and he'll git come up with, one of these days, I says to myself, insulting ghosts that way. They'll stand it for a while, maybe, but they won't stand it always, for anybody that knows about ghosts knows how easy they are hurt, and how revengeful they are.

So we was all quiet and still, Jim and me being scared, and Tom busy. By and by Tom fetched the balloon to a standstill, and says:

"Now get up and look, you sapheads."

We done it, and there was the sure-enough water right under us!—clear, and blue, and cool, and deep, and wavy with the breeze, the loveliest sight that ever was. And all about it was grassy banks, and flowers, and shady groves of big trees, looped together with vines, and all looking so peaceful and comfortable—enough to make a body cry, it was so beautiful.

Jim did cry, and rip and dance and carry on, he was so thankful and out of his mind for joy. It was my watch, so I had to stay by the works, but Tom and Jim clumb down and drank a barrel apiece, and fetched me up a lot, and I've tasted a many a good thing in my life, but nothing that ever begun with that water.

Then we went down and had a swim, and then Tom came up and spelled me, and me and Jim had a swim, and then Jim spelled Tom, and me and Tom had a foot race and a boxing mill, and I don't reckon I ever had such a good time in my life. It warn't so very hot, because it was close on to evening, and we hadn't any clothes on, anyway. Clothes is well enough in school, and in towns, and at balls, too, but there ain't no sense in them when there ain't no civilization nor other kinds of bothers and fussiness around.

"Lion's a-comin'!—lions! Quick, Mars Tom! Jump for yo' life, Huck!"

Oh, and didn't we! We never stopped for clothes, but waltzed up the ladder just so. Jim lost his head straight off—he always done it whenever he got excited and scared; and so now, 'stead of just easing the ladder up from the ground a little, so the animals couldn't reach it, he turned on a raft of power, and we went whizzing up and was dangling in the sky before he got his wits together and seen what a foolish thing he was doing. Then he stopped her, but he had clean forgot what to do next; so there we was, so high that the lions looked like pups, and we was drifting off in the wind.

But Tom he shinned up and went for the works and begun to slant her down, and back toward the lake, where the animals was gathering like a camp meeting, and I judged he had lost his head, too; for he knowed I was too scared to climb, and did he want to dump me among the tigers and things?

But no, his head was level; he knowed what he was about. He swooped down to within thirty or forty feet of the lake, and stopped right over the centre, and sung out:

"Leggo, and drop!"

I done it, and shot down, feet first, and seemed to go about a mile toward the bottom; and when I come up, he says:

"Now lay on your back and float till you're rested and got your pluck back, then I'll dip the ladder in the water and you can climb aboard."

I done it. Now that was ever so smart of Tom, because if he had started off somewheres else to drop down on the sand, the menagerie would 'a' come along, too, and might 'a' kept us hunting a safe place till I got tuckered out and fell.

And all this time the lions and tigers was sorting out the clothes, and trying to divide them up so there would be some for all, but there was a misunderstanding about it somewheres, on account of some of them trying to hog more than their share; so there was another insurrection, and you never see anything like it in the world. There must 'a' been fifty of them, all mixed up together, snorting and roaring and snapping and biting and rearing, legs and tails in the air, and you couldn't tell which was which, and the sand and fur a-flying. And when they got done, some was dead, and some was limping off crippled, and the rest was setting around on the battlefield, some of them licking their sore places and the others looking up at us and seemed to be kind of inviting us to come down and have some fun, but which we didn't want any.

As for the clothes, they warn't any, any more. Every last rag of them was inside of the animals; and not agreeing with them very well, I don't reckoned, for there was considerable many brass buttons on them, and there was knives in the pockets, too, and smoking tobacco, and nails and chalk and marbles and fish-hooks and things. But I wasn't caring. All that was bothering me was, that all we had now was the professor's clothes, a big enough assortment, but not suitable to go into company with, if we came across any, because the britches was as long as tunnels, and the coats and things according. Still, there was everything a tailor needed, and Jim was a kind of jack-legged tailor, and he allowed he could soon trim a suit or two down for us that would answer.

7

Tom Discourses on the Desert

Still, we thought we would drop down there a minute, but on another errand. Most of the professor's cargo of food was put in cans, in the new way that somebody had just invented; the rest was fresh. When you fetch Mississippi beefsteak to the Great Sahara, you want to be particular and stay in the coolish weather. So we reckoned we would drop into the lion market and see how we could make out there.

We hauled in the ladder and dropped down till we were just above the reach of the animals, then we let down a rope with a slip knot in it and hauled up a dead lion, a small tender one, then yanked up a cub tiger. We had to keep the congregation off with the revolver, or they would 'a' took a hand in the proceedings and helped.

We carved off a supply from both, and saved the skins, and hove the rest overboard. Then we baited some of the professor's hooks with the fresh meat and went a-fishing. We stood over the lake just a convenient distance above the water, and catched a lot of the nicest fish you ever see. It was a most amazing good supper we had; lion steak, tiger steak, fresh fish, and hot corn pone. I don't want nothing better than that.

We had some fruit to finish off with. We got it out of the top of a monstrous tree. It was a very slim tree that hadn't a branch on it from the bottom plumb to the top, and there it bursted out like a feather duster. It was a pa'm tree, of course; anybody knows a pa'm tree, the minute he see it, by the pictures. We went for cocoanuts in this one, but there warn't none. There was only big loose branches of things like oversized grapes, and Tom allowed they was dates, because he said they answered the discription in the Arabian Nights and the other books. Of course they mightn't be, and they might be poison; so we had to wait a spell, and watch and see if the birds et them. They done it; so we done it, too, and they was most amazing good.

By this time monstrous big birds begun to come and settle on the dead animals. They was plucky creturs; they would tackle one end of a lion that was being gnawed at the other end by another lion. If the lion drove the bird away, it didn't do no good; he was back again the minute the lion was busy.

The big birds come out of every part of the sky—you could make them out with the glass while they was still so far away you couldn't see them with your naked eye. Tom said the birds didn't find out the meat was there by the smell; they had to find it out by seeing it. Oh, but ain't that an eye for you! Tom said at the distance of five mile a patch of dead lions couldn't look any bigger than a person's fingernail, and he couldn't imagine how the birds could notice sich a little thing so far off.

It was strange and unnatural to see lion eat lion, and we thought maybe they warn't kin. But Jim said that didn't make no difference. He said a hog was fond of her own children, and so was a spider, and reckoned maybe a lion was pretty

near as unprincipled, though maybe not quite.
He thought likely a lion wouldn't eat his own fa-
ther, if he knowed which was him, but reckoned
he would eat his brother-in-law if he was uncommon hungry, and eat his mother-in-law any
time. But reckoning don't settle nothing. You
can reckon till the cows come home, but that
don't fetch you to no decision. So we give it up
and let it drop.

Generally it was very still in the desert nights,
but this time there was music. A lot of other animals come to dinner; sneaking yelpers that Tom
allowed was jackals, and roach-backed ones that
he said was hyenas; and all the whole biling of
them kept up a racket all the time. They made a
picture in the moonlight that was more different
than any picture I ever see. We had a line out and
made fast to the top of a tree, and didn't stand no
watch, but all turned in and slept; but I was up
two or three times to look down at the animals
and hear the music. It was like having a front
seat at a menagerie for nothing, which I hadn't
ever had before, and so it seemed foolish to
sleep and not make the most of it; I mightn't
ever have such a chance again.

We went a-fishing again in the early dawn, and then lazied around all day in the deep shade on an island, taking turn to watch and see that none of the animals came a-snooping around there after erronorts for dinner. We was going to leave the next day, but couldn't, it was too lovely.

The day after, when we rose up toward the sky and sailed off eastward, we looked back and watched that place till it warn't nothing but just a speck in the desert, and I tell you it was like saying goodbye to a friend that you ain't never going to see any more.

Jim was thinking to himself, and at last he says:

"Mars Tom, we's mos' to de end er de desert now, I speck."

"Why?"

"Well, hit stan' to reason we is. You knows how long we's been a-skimmin' over it. Mus' be mos' out o' san'. Hit's a wonder to me dat it's hilt out as long as it has."

"Shucks, there's plenty sand, you needn't worry."

"Oh, I ain't a-worryin', Mars Tom, only

wonderin', dat's all. De Lord's got plenty san', I ain't doubtin' dat; but nemmine, He ain't gwine to was'e it jist on dat account; en I allows dat dis desert's plenty big enough now, jist de way she is, en you can't spread her out no mo' 'dout was' in' san'."

"Oh, go 'long! We ain't much more than fairly started across the desert yet. The United States is a pretty big country, ain't it? Ain't it, Huck?"

"Yes," I says, "there ain't no bigger one, I don't reckon."

"Well," he says, "this desert is about the shape of the United States, and if you was to lay it down on top of the United States, it would cover the land of the free out of sight like a blanket. There'd be a little corner sticking out, up at Maine and away up northwest, and Florida sticking out like a turtle's tail, and that's all. We've took California away from the Mexicans two or three years ago, so that part of the Pacific coast is ours now, and if you laid the Great Sahara down with her edge on the Pacific, she would cover the United States and stick out past New York six hundred miles into the Atlantic Ocean."

I says:

"Good land! Have you got the documents for that, Tom Sawyer?"

"Yes, they're right here, and I've been studying them. You can look for yourself. From New York to the Pacific is 2,600 miles. From one end of the Great Desert to the other is 3,200. The United States contains 3,600,000 square miles, the desert contains 4,162,000. With the desert's bulk you could cover up every last inch of the United States, and in under, where the edges projected out, you could tuck England, Scotland, Ireland, France, Denmark, and all Germany. Yes, sir, you could hide the home of the brave and all them countries clean out of sight under the Great Sahara, and you would still have 2,000 square miles of sand left."

"Well," I says, "it clean beats me. Why Tom, it shows that the Lord took as much pains makin' this desert as makin' the United States and all them other countries."

Jim says: "Huck, dat don' stan' to reason. I reckon dis desert wa'n't made at all. Now you take en look at it like dis—you look at it, and see ef I's right. What's a desert good for? 'Tain't good for nuthin'. Dey ain't no way to make it pay. Hain't dat so, Huck?"

"Yes, I reckon."

"Hain't it so, Mars Tom?"

"I guess so. Go on."

"Ef a thing ain't good, it's made in vain, ain't it?"

"Yes."

"Now, den! Do de Lord make anything in vain? You answer me dat."

"Well—no, He don't."

"Den how come He make a desert?"

"Well, go on. How did He come to make it?"

"Mars Tom, I b'lieve it uz jes like when you's buildin' a house; dey's allays a lot o' truck en rubbish lef' over. What does you do wid it? Doan' you take en k'yart it off en dump it into a ole vacant back lot? 'Course. Now, den its my opinion hit was jest like dat—dat de Great Sahara warn't made at all, she jes' happen'.'"

I said it was a real good argument, and I believe it was the best one Jim ever made. Tom he said the same, but said the trouble about arguments is, ain't nothing but theories, after all, and theories don't prove nothing; they only give you a place to rest on, a spell, when you are tuckered out butting around and around trying to find out something there ain't no way to find out. And he says:

"There's another trouble about theories: there's always a hole in them somewheres, sure, if you look close enough. It's just so with this one of Jim's. Look what billions and billions of stars there is. How does it come that there was just exactly enough star-stuff, and none left over? How does it come there ain't no sand pile up there?"

But Jim was fixed for him and says:

"What's de Milky Way?—dat's what I want to know. What's de Milky Way? Answer me dat!"

In my opinion it was just a sockdologer. It's only an opinion, it's only my opinion and others may think different; but I said it then and I stand to it now—it was a sockdologer. And moreover, besides, it landed Tom Sawyer. He couldn't say a word. He had that stunned look of a person that's been shot in the back with a keg of nails. All he said was, as for people like me and Jim, he'd just as soon have intellectual intercourse with a catfish. But anybody can say that—and notice they always do when somebody has fetched them a lifter. Tom Sawyer was tired of that end of the subject.

So we got back to talking about the size of the desert again, and the more we compared it with this and that and t'other thing, the more nobler and bigger and grander it got to look right along. And so, hunting among the figgers, Tom found, by and by, that it was just the same size as the Empire of China. Then he showed us the spread the Empire of China made on the map, and the room she took up in the world. Well, it was wonderful to think of, and I says:

"Why, I've heard talk about the desert plenty of times, but I never knowed before how important she was."

Then Tom says:

"Important! Sahara important! That's just the way with some people. If a thing's big, it's important. That's all the sense they've got. All they can see is size. Why, look at England. It's the most important country in the world; and yet you could put it in China's vest pocket; and not only that, but you'd have the dicken's own time to find it again the next time you wanted it. And

look at Russia. It spreads all around and everywhere, and yet ain't no more important in this
world than Rhode Island is, and hasn't got half
as much in it that's worth saving."

Away off now we see a little hill, a-standing up
just on the edge of the world. Tom broke off his
talk, and reached for a glass very much excited,
and took a look, and says:

"That's it—it's the one I've been looking for,
sure. If I'm right, it's the one the dervish took
the man into and showed him all the treasures."

So we began to gaze, and he begun to tell
about it out of the Arabian Nights.

8

The Treasure Hill

Tom said it happened like this:

A dervish was stumping it along through the desert, on foot, one blazing hot day, and had come a thousand miles and was pretty poor, and hungry, and ornery and tired, and along about where we are now he ran across a camel driver with a hundred camels, and asked him for some a'ms. But the camel driver he asked to be excused. The dervish said:

"Don't you own these camels?"

"Yes, they're mine."

"Are you in debt?"

"Who—me? No."

"Well, a man who owns a hundred camels and

ain't in debt is rich—and not only rich, but very rich. Ain't it so?"

The camel driver owned up that it was so. Then the dervish says:

"God has made you rich, and He has made me poor. He has His reasons, and they are wise, blessed be His name. But He has willed that His rich shall help the poor, and you have turned away from me, your brother, in my need, and He will remember this, and you will lose by it."

That made the camel driver feel shaky, but all the same he was born hoggish after money and didn't like to let go a cent; so he begun to whine and explain, and said times were hard, and although he had took a full freight down to Balsora and got a fat rate for it, he couldn't git no return freight, so he wasn't making no great things out of his trip. So the dervish starts along again, and says:

"All right, if you want to take the risk; but I reckon you have made a mistake this time, and missed the chance."

Of course the camel driver wanted to know what kind of a chance he had missed, because maybe there was money in it; so he ran after the dervish, and begged him so hard and earnest to take pity on him that at last the dervish gave in, and says:

"Do you see that hill yonder? Well, in that hill is all the treasures of the earth, and I was looking around for a man with a particular good, kind heart and a noble, generous disposition, because if I could find just that man, I've got a kind of a salve I could put in his eyes and he could see the treasures and get them out."

So then the camel driver was in a sweat; and he cried, and begged, and took on, and went down on his knees, and said he was just that kind of man, and said he could fetch a thousand people that would say he warn't ever described so exact before.

"Well, then," says the dervish, "All right. If we load the hundred camels, can I have half of them?"

The driver was so glad he couldn't hardly hold in, and says:

"Now you're shouting."

So they shook hands on the bargain, and the dervish got out his box and rubbed the salve on the driver's eye, and the hill opened and he went in, and there, sure enough, was piles and piles of gold and jewels sparkling like all the stars in the heaven had fell down.

So him and the dervish laid into it, and they loaded every camel till he couldn't carry no more; then they said goodbye, and each of them started off with his fifty. But pretty soon the camel driver came and overtook the dervish and says:

"You ain't in society, you know, and you don't really need all you've got. Won't you be good, and let me have ten of your camels?"

"Well," the dervish says, "I don't know but what you say is reasonable enough."

So he done it, and they separated, and the dervish started off again with his forty. But pretty soon here comes the camel driver bawling after him again, and whines and slobbers around and begs another ten off of him, saying thirty camel-loads of treasure was enough to see a dervish through, because they live very simple, you know, and don't keep house, but board around and give their note.

But that warn't the end yet. That ornery hound kept coming and coming till he had begged back all the camels and had the whole hundred. Then he was satisfied, and ever so grateful, and said he wouldn't ever forgit the dervish as long as he lived, and nobody hadn't been so good to him before, and liberal. So they shook hands good-bye, and separated and started off again.

But do you know, it warn't ten minutes till the camel driver was unsatisfied again—he was the lowdownest reptyle in seven countries—and he came a-running again. And this time the thing he wanted was the dervish to rub some of the salve on his other eye.

"Why?" said the dervish.

"Oh, you know," says the driver.

"Know what?"

"Well, you can't fool me," says the driver. "You're trying to keep back something from me, you know it mighty well. You know, I reckon, that if I had the salve on the other eye I could see a lot more things that's valuable. Come—please put it on."

The dervish says:

"I wasn't keeping anything back from you. I don't mind telling you what would happen if I put it on. You'd never see again. You'd be stone-blind the rest of your days."

But do you know that beat wouldn't believe him. No, he begged and begged, and whined and cried, till at last the dervish opened his box and told him to put it on, if he wanted to. So the man done it, and, sure enough, he was blind as a bat in a minute.

Then the dervish laughed at him and mocked at him and made fun of him, and says:

"Goodbye—a man that's blind hain't got no use for jewellery."

And he cleared out with the hundred camels, and left that man to wander around poor and miserable and friendless the rest of his days in the desert.

Jim said he'd bet it was a lesson to him.

"Yes," Tom says, "and like a considerable many lessons a body gets. They ain't no account, because the thing don't ever happen the same way again—and can't. The time Hen Scovil fell down the chimbly and crippled his back for life, everybody said it would be a lesson to him. What kind of lesson? How was he going to use it? He couldn't climb chimblies no more, and he hadn't no more backs to break."

"All de same, Mars Tom, dey is sich a thing as

learnin' by expe'ence. De Good Book say de burnt chile shun de fire."

"Well, I ain't denying that a thing's a lesson if it's a thing that can happen twice just the same way. There's lots of such things, and they educate a person, that's what Uncle Abner always said; but there's forty million lots of the other kind—that kind that don't happen the same way twice—and they ain't no real use, they ain't no more instructive than the smallpox. When you've got it, it ain't no good to find out you ought to been vaccinated, and it ain't no good to git vaccinated afterward, because the smallpox don't come but once. But on the other hand, Uncle Abner said that the person that had took a bull by the tail once had learnt sixty or seventy times as much as a person that hadn't, and said a person that started in to carry a cat home by the tail was gitting knowledge that was always going to be useful to him, and warn't ever going to grow dim or doubtful. But I can tell you, Jim, Uncle Abner was down on them people that's all the time trying to dig a lesson out of everything that happens, no matter whether—"

But Jim was asleep. Tom looked kind of

ashamed, because you know a person always feels bad when he is talking uncommon fine and thinks the other person is admiring, and that other person goes to sleep that way. Of course he oughtn't to go to sleep, because it's shabby; but the finer a person talks the certainer it is to make you sleep, and so when you come to look at it it ain't nobody's fault in particular; both of them's to blame.

Jim began to snore—soft and blubbery at first, then a long rasp, then a stronger one, then a half a dozen horrible ones, like the last water sucking down the plughole of a bathtub, then the same with more power to it, and some big coughs and snorts flung in, the way a cow does that is choking to death; and when the person has got to that point he is at his level best, and can wake up a man that is in the next block with a dipperful of loddanum in him, but can't wake himself up although all that awful noise of his'n ain't but three inches from his own ears. And that is the curiousest thing in the world, seems to me. But you rake a match to light the candle, and that little bit of a noise will fetch him. I wish I knowed what was the reason of that, but there don't seem

to be no way to find out. Now there was Jim
alarming the whole desert, and yanking the animals out, for miles and miles around, to see
what in the nation was going on up there; there
warn't nobody nor nothing that was as close to
the noise as he was, and yet he was the only
cretur that wasn't disturbed by it. We yelled at
him and whooped at him, it never done no good;
but the first time there come a little wee noise
that wasn't of a usual kind, it woke him up. No,
sir, I've thought it all over, and so has Tom, and
there ain't no way to find out why a snorer can't
hear himself snore.

Jim said he hadn't been asleep; he just shut his
eyes so he could listen better.

Tom said nobody warn't accusing him.

That made him look like he wished he hadn't
said anything. And he wanted to git away from
the subject, I reckon, because he begun to abuse
the camel driver, just the way a person does
when he has got catched in something and
wants to take it out of somebody else. He let
into the camel driver the hardest he knowed
how, and I had to agree with him; and he praised
up the dervish the highest he could, and I had to

agree with him there, too. But Tom says:

"I ain't so sure. You call that dervish so dreadful liberal and good and unselfish, but I don't quite see it. He didn't hunt up another poor dervish, did he? No, he didn't. If he was so unselfish, why didn't he go in there himself and take a pocketful of jewels and go along and be satisfied? No, sir, the person he was hunting for was a man with a hundred camels. He wanted to get away with all the treasure he could."

"Why, Mars Tom, he was willin' to divide, fair and square; he only struck for fifty camels."

"Because he knowed how he was going to git all of them by and by."

"Mars Tom, he tole de man de truck would make him bline."

"Yes, because he knowed the man's character. It was just the kind of man he was hunting for— a man that never believes anybody's word or anybody's honourableness, because he ain't got none of his own. I reckon there's lots of people like that dervish. They swindle, right and left, but they always make the other person seem to swindle himself. They keep inside of the letter of the law all the time, and there ain't no way to

git hold of them. They don't put the salve on—
oh, no, that would be sin; but they know how to
fool you into putting it on, then it's you that
blinds yourself. I reckon the dervish and the
camel driver was just a pair—a fine, smart,
brainy rascal, and a dull, coarse, ignorant one,
but both of them rascals, just the same."

"Mars Tom, does you reckon dey's any o' dat
kind o' salve in de worl' now?"

"Yes, Uncle Abner says there is. He says
they've got it in New York, and they put it on the
country people's eyes and shows them all the
railroads in the world, and they go in and git
them, and then when they rub the salve on the
other eye the other man bids them goodbye and
goes off with their railroads. Here's the treasure
hill now. Lower away!"

We landed, but it warn't as interesting as I
thought it was going to be, because we couldn't
find the place where they went in to git the treasure. Still, it was plenty interesting enough, just
to see the mere hill itself where such a wonderful thing happened. Jim said he wouldn't 'a'
missed it for three dollars, and I felt the same
way.

And to me and Jim, as wonderful a thing as any was the way Tom could come into a strange big country like this and go straight and find a little hump like that and tell it in a minute from a million other humps that was almost just like it, and nothing to help him but only his own learning and his own natural smartness. We talked it over together, but couldn't make out how he done it. He had the best head on him I ever see; and all he lacked was age to make a name for himself equal to Captain Kidd or George Washington. I bet you it would 'a crowded either of them to find that hill, with all their gifts, but it warn't nothing to Tom Sawyer; he went across Sahara and put his finger on it as easy as you could pick a monkey out of a bunch of angels.

We found a pond of salt water close by and scraped up a raft of salt around the edges, and loaded up the lion's skin and the tiger's so as they would keep till Jim could tan them.

9

The Sandstorm

We went a-fooling along for a day or two, and
then just as the full moon was touching the
ground on the other side of the desert, we see a
string of little black figgers moving across its
big silver face. You could see them as plain as if
they was painted on the moon with ink. It was
another caravan. We cooled down our speed and
tagged along after it, just to have company,
though it warn't going our way. It was a rattler,
that caravan, and a most bully sight to look at
next morning when the sun came a-streaming
across the desert and flung the long shadders of
the camels on the gold sand like a thousand
granddaddy-longlegses marching in procession.

We never went very near it, because we knowed
better now than to act like that and scare people's camels and break up their caravans. It was
the gayest outfit you ever see, for rich clothes
and nobby style. Some of the chiefs rose on
dromedaries, the first we ever see, and very tall,
and they go plunging along like they was on
stilts, and they rock the man that is on them pretty violent and churn up his dinner considerable,
I bet you, but they make noble good time, and a
camel ain't nowheres with them for speed.

The caravan camped, during the middle part of
the day, and then started again about the middle
of the afternoon. Before long the sun began to
look very curious. First it kind of turned to
brass, and then copper, and after that it began to
look like a blood-red ball, and the air got hot and
close, and pretty soon all the sky in the west
darkened up and looked thick and foggy, but
fiery and dreadful—like it looks through a piece
of red glass, you know. We looked down and see
a big confusion going on in the caravan, and a
rushing every which way like they was scared;
and then they all flopped down in the sand and
laid there perfectly still.

Pretty soon we see something coming that stood up like an amazing wide wall, and reached from the desert up into the sky and hid the sun, and it was coming like the nation, too. Then a little faint breeze struck us, and then it came harder, and grains of sand begun to sift against our faces and sting like fire, and Tom sung out:

"It's a sandstorm—turn your backs to it!"

We done it; and in another minute it was blowing a gale, and the sand beat against us by the shovelful, and the air was so thick with it we couldn't see a thing. In five minutes the boat was level full, and we was setting on the lockers buried up to the chin in sand, and only our heads out and could hardly breathe.

Then the storm thinned, and we see that monstrous wall go a-sailing off across the desert, awful to look at, I tell you. We dug ourselves out and looked down, and where the caravan was before there wasn't anything but just the sand ocean now, and still and quiet. All them people and camels was smothered and dead and buried—buried under ten foot of sand, we reckoned, and Tom allowed it might be years before the wind uncovered them, and all that time their friends wouldn't ever know what become of that caravan. Tom said:

"Now we know what happened to the people we got the swords and pistols from."

Yes, sir, that was just it. It was as plain as day now. They got buried in the sandstorm, and the wild animals couldn't get at them, and the wind never uncovered them again until they was dried to leather and warn't fit to eat. It seemed to me we had felt as sorry for them people as a person could for anybody, and as mournful, too, but we was mistaken; the last caravan's death went harder with us, a good deal harder. You see, the others was total strangers, and we never got to feeling acquainted with them at all, except, maybe, a little with the man that was watching the girl, but it was different with the last caravan. We was huvvering around them the whole night and 'most a whole day, and had got to feeling real friendly with them, and acquainted. I have found out that there ain't no surer way to find out whether you like people or hate people than to travel with them. Just so with these. We kind of liked them from the start, and travelling with them put on the finisher. The longer we

travelled with them, the more we got used to
their ways, the better and better we liked them,
and the gladder and gladder we was that we run
across them. We had come to know some of
them so well that we called them by name when
we was talking about them, and soon got so fa-
miliar and sociable that we even dropped the
Miss and Mister and just called their plain
names without any handle, and it did not seem
unpolite, but just the right thing. Of course, it
wasn't their own names, but names we give
them. There was Mr Elexander Robinson and
Miss Adeline Robinson, and Colonel Jacob
McDougal and Miss Harryet McDougal, and
Judge Jeremiah Butler and young Bushrod Butler, and these was big chiefs mostly that wore
splendid great turbans and simmeters, and
dressed like the Grand Mogul, and their fami-
lies. But as soon as we come to know them
good, and like them very much, it warn't Mister,
nor Judge, nor nothing, any more, but only
Elleck, and Addy, and Jake, and Hattie, and
Jerry, and Buck, and so on.

And you know the more you join in with people in their joys and their sorrows, the more

nearer and dearer they come to be to you. Now
we warn't cold and indifferent, the way most
travellers is, we was right down friendly and sociable, and took a chance in everything that was
going, and the caravan could depend on us to be
on hand every time, it didn't make no difference
what it was.

When they camped, we camped right over
them, ten or twelve feet up in the air. When they
et a meal, we et ourn, and it made it ever so
much homeliker to have their company. When
they had a wedding that night, and Buck and
Addy got married, we got ourselves up in the
very starchiest of the professor's duds for the
blowout, and when they danced we jined in and
shook a foot up there.

But it is sorrow and trouble that brings you the
nearest, and it was a funeral that done it with us.
It was next morning, just in the still of dawn. We
didn't know the diseased, and he warn't in our
set, but that never made no difference; he be-
longed to the caravan, and that was enough, and
there warn't no more sincere tears shed over him
than the ones we dripped on him from up there
eleven hundred foot on high.

Yes, parting with this caravan was much more bitterer than it was to part with them others, which was comparative strangers, and been dead so long, anyway. We had knowed these in their lives, and was fond of them, too, and now to have death snatch them from right before our faces while we was looking, and leave us so lonesome and friendless in the middle of that big desert, it did hurt so, and we wished we mightn't ever make any more friends on that voyage if we was going to lose them again like that.

We couldn't keep from talking about them, and they was all the time coming up in our memory, and looking just the way they looked when we was all alive and happy together. We could see the line marching, and the shiny spearheads a-winking in the sun; we could see the dromedaries lumbering along; we could see the wedding and the funeral; and more oftener than anything else we could see them praying, because they don't allow nothing to prevent that; whenever the call come, several times a day, they would stop right there, and stand up and face to the east, and lift back their heads, and spread out their arms and begin, and four or five times they would go down on their knees, and then fall forward and touch their forehead to the ground.

Well, it warn't good to go on talking about them, lovely as they was in their life, and dear to us in their life and death both, because it didn't do no good, and made us too downhearted. Jim allowed he was going to live as good a life as he could, so he could see them again in a better world; and Tom kept still and didn't tell him they was Mohammedans; it warn't no use to disappoint him, he was feeling bad enough just as it was.

When we woke up next morning we was feeling a little cheerfuler, and had had a most powerful good sleep, because sand is the comfortest bed there is, and I don't see why people that can afford it don't have it more. And it's terrible good ballast, too; I never see the balloon so steady before.

Tom allowed we had twenty tons of it, and wondered what we better do with it; it was good sand, and it didn't seem good sense to throw it away. Jim says:

"Mars Tom, can't we tote it back home en sell it? How long'll it take?"

"Depends on the way we go."

"Well, sah, she's wuth a quarter of a dollar a load at home, en I reckon we's got as much as twenty loads, hain't we? How much would dat be?"

"Five dollars."

"By jings, Mars Tom, le's shove for home right on de spot! Hit's more'n a dollar en a half apiece, hain't it?"

"Yes."

"Well, ef dat ain't makin' money de easiest ever I struck! She jes' rained in—never cos' us a lick o' work. Le's mosey right along, Mars Tom."

But Tom was thinking and ciphering away so busy and excited he never heard him. Pretty soon he says:

"Five dollars—sho! Look here, this sand's worth—worth—why, it's worth no end of money."

"How is dat, Mars Tom? Go on, honey, go on!"

"Well, the minute people knows it's genuwyne sand from the genuwyne Desert of Sahara, they'll just be in a perfect state of mind to git hold of some of it to keep on the whatnot in a vial with a label on it for curiosity. All we got to do is to put it up in vials and float around all over the United States and peddle them out at ten cents apiece. We've got all of ten thousand dollars' worth of sand in this boat."

Me and Jim went all to pieces with joy, and begun to shout whoopjamboreehoo, and Tom says:

"And we can keep on coming back and fetching sand, and coming back and fetching more sand, and just keep it a-going till we've carted this whole desert over there and sold it out; and there ain't ever going to be any opposition, either, because we'll take out a patent."

"My goodness," I says, "we'll be as rich as Creosote, won't we, Tom?"

"Yes—Creesus, you mean. Why, that dervish was hunting in that hill of treasures of the earth, and didn't know he was walking over the real ones for a thousand miles. He was blinder than he made the driver."

"Mars Tom, how much is we gwyne to be worth?"

"Well, I don't know yet. It's got to be ciphered, and it ain't the easiest job to do, either, because it's over four million square miles of sand at ten cents a vial."

Jim was awful excited, but this faded it out considerable, and he shook his head and says:

"Mars Tom, we can't 'ford all dem vials—a king couldn't. We better not try to take de whole desert, Mars Tom, de vials gwyne to bust us, sho'."

Tom's excitement died out, too, now, and I reckoned it was on account of the vials, but it wasn't. He set there thinking, and got bluer and bluer, and at last he says:

"Boys, it won't work; we got to give it up."

"Why, Tom?"

"On account of the duties."

I couldn't make nothing out of that, neither could Jim. I says:

"What is our duty, Tom? Because if we can't git around it, why can't we just do it? People often has to."

But he says:

"Oh, it ain't that kind of duty. The kind I mean is a tax. Whenever you strike a frontier—that's the border of a country, you know—you find a custom house there, and the gov'ment officers comes and rummages among your things and charges a big tax, which they call a duty because it's their duty to bust you if they can, and if you don't pay the duty they'll hog your sand. They call if confiscating, but that don't deceive nobody, it's just hogging, and that's all it is. Now if we try to carry this sand home the way we're pointed now, we got to climb fences till we git tired—just frontier after frontier—Egypt, Arabia, Hindustan, and so you see, easy enough, we can't go that road."

"Why, Tom," I says, "we can sail right over their old frontiers; how are they going to stop us?"

He looked sorrowful at him, and says, very grave:

"Huck Finn, do you think that would be honest?"

I hate them kind of interruptions. I never said nothing, and he went on:

"Well, we're shut off the other way, too. If we go back the way we've come, there's the New York custom house, and that is worse than all of them put together, on account of the kind of cargo we've got."

"Why?"

"Well, they can't raise Sahara sand in America, of course, and when they can't raise a thing there, the duty is fourteen hundred thousand per cent on it if you try to fetch it in from where they do raise it."

"There ain't no sense in that, Tom Sawyer."

"Who said there was? What do you talk to me like that for, Huck Finn? You wait till I say a thing's got sense in it before you go to accusing me of saying it."

"All right, consider me crying about it, and sorry. Go on."

Jim says:

"Mars Tom, do dey jam dat duty onto everything we can't raise in America, en don't make no 'stinction 'twixt anything?"

"Yes, that's what they do."

"Mars Tom, ain't de blessin' o' de Lord de mos' valuable thing dey is?"

"Yes, it is."

"Don't de preacher stan' up in de pulpit en call it down on de people?"

"Yes."

"Whah do it come from?"

"From heaven."

"Yassir! You's jes' right, 'deed you is, honey—it come from heaven, en dat's a foreign country. Now, den! Do dey put a tax on dat blessin'?"

"No, they don't."

" 'Course dey don't; en so it stan' to reason dat you's mistaken, Mars Tom. Dey wouldn't put de tax on po' truck like san', dat everybody ain't 'bleeged to have, en leave it off'n de bes' thing dey is, which nobody can't git along widout."

Tom Sawyer was stumped; he see Jim had got him where he couldn't budge. He tried to wiggle out by saying they had forgot to put on that tax, but they'd be sure to remember about it, next season of Congress, and then they'd put it on, but that was a poor lame come-off, and he knowed it. He said there warn't nothing foreign that warn't taxed but just that one, and so they couldn't be consistent without taxing it, and to be consistent was the first law of politics. So he stuck to it that they'd left it out unintentional and would be certain to do their best to fix it before they got caught and laughed at.

But I didn't feel no more interest in such

things, as long as we couldn't git our sand
through, and it made me low-spirited, and Jim
the same. Tom he tried to cheer us up by saying
he would think up another speculation for us
that would be just as good as this one and better, but it didn't do no good, we didn't believe
there was any as big as this. It was mighty hard;
such a little while ago we was so rich, and could
'a' bought a country and started a kingdom and
been celebrated and happy, and now we was so
poor and ornery again, and had our sand left on
our hands. The sand was looking so lovely before, just like gold and di'monds, and the feel of
it was so soft and so silky and nice, but now I
couldn't bear the sight if it, it made me sick to
look at it, and I knowed I wouldn't ever feel
comfortable again till we got shut of it, and I
didn't have it there no more to remind us of what
we had been and what we had got degraded down
to. The others was feeling the same way about it
that I was. I knowed it, because they cheered up
so, the minute I says le's throw this truck overboard.

Well, it was going to be work, you know, and
pretty solid work, too; so Tom he divided it up

according to fairness and strength. He said me and him would clear out a fifth apiece of the sand, and Jim three-fifths. Jim he didn't quite like that agreement. He says:

"'Course I's de stronges', en I's willin' to do a share accordin', but jings you's kinder pilin' it into ole Jim, Mars Tom, hain't you?"

"Well, I didn't think so, Jim, but you try your hand at fixing it, and let's see."

So Jim reckoned it wouldn't be no more than fair if me and Tom done a tenth apiece. Tom he turned his back to git room and be private, and then he smole a smile that spread around and covered the whole Sahara to the westward, back to the Atlantic edge of it where we come from. Then he turned around again and said it was a good enough arrangement, and we was satisfied if Jim was. Jim said he was.

So then Tom measured off our two-tenths in the bow and left the rest for Jim, and it surprised Jim a good deal to see how much difference there was and what a raging lot of sand his share came to, and said he was powerful glad now that he had spoke up in time and got the first arrangement altered, for he said that even the way it was now, there was more sand than enjoyment in his end of the contract, he believed.

Then we laid into it. It was mighty hot work, and tough; so hot we had to move up into cooler weather or we couldn't 'a' stood it. Me and Tom took turn about, and one worked while t'other rested, but there warn't nobody to spell poor old Jim, and he made all that part of Africa damp, he sweated so. We couldn't work good, we was so full of laugh, and Jim he kept fretting and wanting to know what tickled us so, and we had to keep making up things to account for it, and they was pretty poor inventions, but they done well enough, Jim didn't see through them. At last when we got done we was 'most dead, but not with work but with laughing. By and by Jim was 'most dead, too, but it was with work; then we took turns and spelled him, and he was as thankful as he could be, and would set on the gunnel and swab the sweat, and heave and pant, and say how good we was to him, and he wouldn't ever forgit us. He was always the greatfulest person I ever see, for any little thing you done for him.

10

Jim Standing Siege

The next few meals was pretty sandy, but that
don't make no difference when you are hungry;
and when you ain't it ain't no satisfaction to eat,
anyway, and so a little grit in the meat ain't no
particular drawback, as far as I can see.

Then we struck the east end of the desert at
last, sailing on a northeast course. Away off on
the edge of the sand, in a soft pinky light, we see
three little sharp roofs like tents, and Tom says:

"It's the pyramids of Egypt."

It made my heart fairly jumpy. You see, I had
seen a many and a many picture of them, and
heard tell of them a hundred times, and yet to
come on them all of a sudden, that way, and find
they was real, 'stead of imaginations, 'most
knocked the breath out of me with surprise. It's a

curious thing, that the more you hear about a
grand and big and bully thing or person, the
more it kind of dreamies out, as you may say,
and gets to be a big dim wavy figger made out of
moonshine and nothing solid to it. It's just so
with George Washington, and the same with
them pyramids.

And moreover, besides the thing they always
said about them seemed to me to be stretchers.
There was a feller come to the Sunday school
once, and had a picture of them, and made a
speech, and said the biggest pyramid covered
thirteen acres, and was 'most five hundred foot
high, just a steep mountain, all built out of hunks
of stone as big as a bureau, and laid up in perfectly regular layers, like stair steps. Thirteen
acres, you see, for just one building; it's a farm.
If it hadn't been in Sunday school I would 'a'
judged it was a lie; and outside I was certain of
it. And he said there was a hole in the pyramid,
and you could go there with candles, and go ever
so far up a long slanting tunnel, and come to a
large room in the stomach of that stone mountain, and there you would find a big stone chest
with a king in it, four thousand years old. I said

to myself, then, if that ain't a lie I will eat the king if they will fetch him, for even Methusalem warn't that old, and nobody claims it.

As we come a little nearer we see the yaller sand come to an end in a long straight edge like a blanket, and onto it was joined, edge to edge, a wide country of bright green, with a snakey stripe crooking through it, and Tom said it was the Nile. It made my heart jump again, for the Nile was another thing that wasn't real to me. Now I can tell you one thing which is dead certain; if you will fool along over three thousand miles of yaller sand, all glimmering with heat so that it makes your eyes water to look at it, and you've been a considerable part of a week doing it, the green country will look so like home and heaven to you that it will make your eyes water again.

It was just so with me, and the same with Jim.

And when Jim got so he could believe it was the land of Egypt he was looking at, he wouldn't enter it standing up, but got down on his knees and took off his hat, because he said it wasn't fitten' for a humble poor feller to come any other way where such men had been as Moses

and Joseph and Pharaoh and the other prophets.
He was a Presbyterian, and had a most deep re-
spect for Moses, which was a Presbyterian, too,
he said. He was all stirred up, and says:

"Hit's de lan' of Egypt, de lan' of Egypt, en I's
'lowed to look at it wid my own eyes! En dah's
de river dat was turn' to blood, en I's looking at
de very same groun' whah de plagues was, en de
lice, en de frogs, en de locus', en de hail, en
whah dey marked de doorpos', en de angel o' de
Lord come by in de darkness o' de night en slew
de fust-born in all de lan' o' Egypt. Ole Jim ain't
worthy to see dis day!"

And then he just broke down and cried, he was
so thankful. So between him and Tom there was
talk enough, Jim being excited because the land
was so full of history—Joseph and his brethren,
Moses in the bulrushers, Jacob coming down
into Egypt to buy corn, the silver cup in the sack,
and all them interesting things; and Tom just as
excited too, because the land was so full of history that was in his line, about Noureddin, and
Bedreddin, and such like monstrous giants, that
made Jim's hair rise, and a raft of other Arabian
Nights folks, which the half of them never done

the things they let on they done, I didn't believe.

Then we struck a disappointment, for one of them early morning fogs started up, and it warn't no use to sail over the top of it, because we would go by Egypt sure, so we judged it was best to set her compass straight for the place where the pyramids was gitting blurred and blotted out, and then drop low and skim along pretty close to the ground and keep a sharp lookout. Tom took the hellum, I stood by to let go the anchor, and Jim he straddled the bow to dig through the fog with his eyes and watch out for danger ahead. We went along a steady gait, but not very fast, and the fog got solider and solider, so solid that Jim looked dim an ragged and smoky through it. It was awful still, and we talked low and was anxious. Now and then Jim would say:

"Highst her a p'int, Mars Tom, highst her!" and up she would skip, a foot or two, and we would slide right over a flat-roofed mud cabin, with people that had been asleep on it just beginning to turn out and gap and stretch; and once when a feller was clear up on his hind legs so he could gap and stretch better, we took him a blip

in the back and knocked him off. By and by, after about an hour, and everything dead still and
we a-straining our ears for sounds and holding
our breath, the fog thinned a little, very sudden,
and Jim sung out in an awful scare:

"Oh, ford e lan's sake, set her back, Mars Tom,
here's de biggest giant outen de 'Rabian Nights
a-comin' for us!" and he went over backwards
in the boat.

Tom slammed on the back-action, and as we
slowed to a standstill a man's face as big as our
house at home looked in over the gunnel, same
as a house looks out of its windows, and I laid
down and died. I must 'a' been clear dead and
gone for as much as a minute or more; then I
come to, and Tom had hitched a boathook onto
the lower lip of the giant and was holding the
balloon steady with it whilst he canted his head
back and got a good long look up at that awful
face.

Jim was on his knees with his hands clasped,
gazing up at the thing in a begging way, and
working his lips, but not getting anything out. I
took only just a glimpse, and was fading out
again, but Tom says:

"He ain't alive, you fools; it's the Sphinx!"

I never see Tom look so little and like a fly; but that was because the giant's head was so big and awful. Awful, yes, so it was, but not dreadful any more, because you could see it was a noble face, and kind of sad, and not thinking about you, but about other things and larger. It was stone, reddish stone, and its nose and ears battered, and that gave it an abused look, and you felt sorrier for it for that.

We stood off a piece, and sailed around it and over it, and it was just grand. It was a man's head, or maybe a woman's, on a tiger's body a hundred and twenty-five foot long, and there was a dear little temple between its front paws. All but the head used to be under the sand, for hundreds of years, maybe thousands, but they had just lately dug the sand away and found that little temple. It took a power of sand to bury that cretur; 'most as much as it would to bury a steamboat, I reckon.

We landed Jim on top of the head, with an American flag to protect him, it being a foreign land; then we sailed off to this and that and t'other distance, to git what Tom called effects

and perspectives and proportions, and Jim he
done the best he could, striking all the different
kinds of attitudes and positions he could study
up, but standing on his head and working his
legs the way a frog does was the best. The further we got away, the littler Jim got, and the
grander the Sphinx got, till at last it was only a
clothes pin on a dome, as you might say. That's
the way perspective brings out the correct proportions, Tom said; he said Julus Cesar's people
didn't know how big he was, they was too close
to him.

Then we sailed off further and further, till we
couldn't see Jim at all any more, and then that
great figger was at its noblest, a-gazing out over
the Nile Valley so still and solemn and lonesome, and all the little shabby huts and things
that was scattered about it clean disappeared and
gone, and nothing around it now but a soft wide
spread of yaller velvet, which was the sand.

That was the right place to stop, and we done
it. We set there a-looking and a-thinking for a
half an hour, nobody a-saying anything, for it
made us feel quiet and kind of solemn to remember it had been looking over that valley just

that same way, and thinking its awful thoughts all to itself for thousands of years, and nobody can't find out what they are to this day.

At last I took up the glasses and see some little black things a-capering around on that velvet carpet, and some more a-climbing up the cretur's back, and then I see two or three wee puffs of white smoke, and told Tom to look. He done it, and says:

"They're bugs. No—hold on; they—why, I believe they're men. Yes, it's men—men and horses both. They're hauling a long ladder up onto the Sphinx's back—now ain't that odd? And they're trying to lean it up a—there's some more puffs of smoke—it's guns! Huck, they're after Jim."

We clapped on the power, and went for them a-biling. We was there in no time, and come a-whizzing down amongst them, and they broke and scattered every which way, and some that was climbing the ladders after Jim let go all holts and fell. We soared up and found him laying on top of the head panting and most tuckered out, partly from howling for help and partly from scare. He had been standing a siege a long time—a week, he said, but it warn't so, it only just seemed so to him because they was crowding him so. They had shot at him, and rained the bullets all around him, but he warn't hit, and when they found he wouldn't stand up and the bullets couldn't git at him when he was laying down, they went for the ladder, and then he knowed it was all up with him if we didn't come pretty quick. Tom was very indignant, and asked him why he didn't show the flag and command them to git, in the name of the United States. Jim said he done it, but they never paid no attention. Tom said he would have this thing looked into at Washington, and says:

"You'll see that they'll have to apologize for insulting the flag, and pay indemnity, too, on top of it, even if they git off that easy."

Jim says:

"What is an indemnity, Mars Tom?"

"It's cash, that's what it is."

"Who gits it, Mars Tom?"

"Why, we do."

"En who gits de apology?"

"The United States. Or, we can take whichever we please. We can take the apology, if we want to, and let the gov'ment take the money."

"How much money will it be, Mars Tom?"

"Well, in an aggravated case like this one, it will be at least three dollars apiece, and I don't know but more."

"Well, den, we'll take the money, Mars Tom, blame de 'pology. Hain't dat ho' notion, too? En hain't it yourn, Huck?"

We talked it over a little and allowed that that was as good a way as any, so we agreed to take the money. It was a new business to me, and I asked Tom if countries always apologized when they had done wrong, and he says:

"Yes; the little ones does."

We was sailing around examining the pyramids, you know, and now we soared up and roosted on the flat top of the biggest one, and found it was just like what the man said in the Sunday school. It was like four pairs of stairs that start broad at the bottom and slants up and comes together in a point at the top, only these stair steps couldn't be clumb the way you climb other stairs; no, for each step was as high as your chin, and you have to be boosted up from behind. The two other pyramids warn't far away,

and the people moving about on the sand between looked like bugs crawling, we was so
high above them.

Tom he couldn't hold himself he was so
worked up with gladness and astonishment to be
in such a celebrated place, and he just dripped
history from every pore, seemed to me. He said
he couldn't scarcely believe he was standing on
the very identical spot the prince flew from on
the bronze horse. It was in the Arabian Nights'
times, he said. Somebody give the prince the
bronze horse with a peg in its shoulder, and he
could git on him and fly through the air like a
bird, and go all over the world, and steer it by
turning the peg, and fly high or low and land
wherever he wanted to.

When he got done telling it there was one of
them uncomfortable silences that comes, you
know, when a person has been telling a whopper
and you feel sorry for him and wish you could
think of some way to change the subject and let
him down easy, but git stuck and don't see no
way, and before you can pull your mind together
and do something, that silence has got in and
spread itself and done the business. I was embar-

rassed, Jim he was embarrassed, and neither of us couldn't say a word. Well, Tom he glowered at me a minute, and says:

"Come, out with it. What do you think?"

I says:

"Tom Sawyer, you don't believe that, yourself."

"What's the reason I don't? What's to hender me?"

"There's one thing to hender you: it can't happen, that's all."

"What's the reason it couldn't happen?"

"You tell me the reason it could happen."

"This balloon is a good enough reason it could happen, I should reckon."

"Why is it?"

"Why is it? I never saw such an idiot. Ain't this balloon and the bronze horse the same thing under different names?"

"No, they're not. One is a balloon and the other's a horse. It's very different. Next you'll be saying a house and a cow is the same thing."

"By Jackson, Huck's got him ag'in! Dey ain't no wigglin' outer dat!"

"Shut your head, Jim; you don't know what

you're talking about. And Huck don't. Look here, Huck, I'll make it plain to you, so you can understand. You see, it ain't the mere form that's got anything to do with their being similar or unsimilar, it's the principle involved; and the principle is the same in both. Don't you see, now?"

I turned it over in my mind, and says:

"Tom, it ain't no use. Principles is all very well but they don't git around that one big fact, that the thing that a balloon can do ain't no sort of proof of what a horse can do."

"Shucks, Huck, you don't get the idea at all. Now look here a minute—it's perfectly plain. Don't we fly through the air?"

"Yes."

"Very well. Don't we fly high or low, just as we please?"

"Yes."

"Don't we steer whichever way we want to?"

"Yes."

"And don't we land when and where we please?"

"Yes."

"How do we move the balloon and steer it?"

"By touching the buttons."

"Now I reckon the thing is clear to you at last. In the other case the moving and steering was done by turning a peg. We touch a button, the prince turned a peg. There ain't an atom of difference, you see. I knowed I could git it through your head if I stuck to it long enough."

He felt so happy he began to whistle. But me and Jim was silent, so he broke off surprised, and says:

"Looky here, Huck Finn, don't you see it yet?"

I says:

"Tom Sawyer, I want to ask you some questions."

"Go ahead," he says, and I see Jim chirk up to listen.

"As I understand it, the whole thing is in the buttons and the peg—the rest ain't of no consequence. A button is one shape, a peg is another shape, but that ain't any matter?"

"No, that ain't any matter, as long as they've both got the same power."

"All right, then. What is the power that's in a candle and in a match?"

"It's the fire."

"It's the same in both, then?"

"Yes, just the same in both."

"All right. Suppose I set fire to a carpenter shop with a match, what will happen to that carpenter shop?"

"She'll burn up."

"And suppose I set fire to this pyramid with a candle—will she burn up?"

"Of course she won't."

"All right. Now the fire's the same, both times. Why does the shop burn, and the pyramid don't?"

"Because the pyramid can't burn."

"Ah! and a horse can't fly!"

"My lan', ef Huck ain't got him ag'in! Huck's landed him high en dry dis time, I tell you! Hit's de smartes' trap I ever see a body walk inter—en ef I—"

But Jim was so full of laugh he got to strangling and couldn't go on, and Tom was that mad to see how neat I had floored him, and turned his own argument ag'in him and knocked him all to rags and flinders with it, that all he could manage to say was that whenever he heard me and Jim try to argue it made him ashamed of the hu-

man race. I never said nothing; I was feeling
pretty well satisfied. When I have got the best of
a person that way, it ain't my way to go around
crowing about it the way some people does, for I
consider that if I was in his place I wouldn't
wish him to crow over me. It's better to be generous, that's what I think.

11

Going for Tom's Pipe

By and by we left Jim to float around in the
neighbourhood of the pyramids, and we clumb
down to the hole where you go into the tunnel,
and went in with some Arabs and candles, and
away in there in the middle of the pyramid we
found a room and a big stone box in it where
they used to keep that king, just as the man in the
Sunday school said; but he was gone, now;
somebody had got him. But I didn't take no interest in the place, because there could be ghosts
there, of course; not fresh ones, but I don't like
no kind.

So then we come out and got some little donkeys and rode a piece, and then went in a boat
another piece, and then more donkeys, and got

to Cairo; and all the way the road was as smooth and beautiful a road as ever I see, and had tall date pa'ms on both sides, and naked children everywhere, and the men was as red as copper, and fine and strong and handsome. And the city was a curiosity. Such narrow streets—why, they were just lanes, and crowded with people with turbans, and women with veils, and everybody rigged out in blazing bright clothes and all sorts of colours, and you wondered how the camels and the people got by each other in such narrow little cracks, but they done it—a perfect jam, you see, and everybody noisy. The stores warn't big enough to turn around in, but you don't have to go in; the storekeeper sat tailor fashion on his counter, smoking his snaky long pipe, and had his things where he could reach them to sell, and he was just as good as in the street, for the camel loads rushed him as they went by.

Now and then a grand person flew by in a carriage with fancy dressed men running and yelling in front of it and whacking anybody with a long rod that didn't get out of the way. And by and by along comes the Sultan riding horseback at the head of a procession, and fairly took your

breath away, his clothes was so splendid; and
everybody fell flat and laid on his stomach while
he went by. I forgot, but a feller helped me to remember. He was one that had a rod and run in
front.

There was churches, but they don't know
enough to keep Sunday; they keep Friday and
break the Sabbath. You have to take off your
shoes when you go in. There was crowds of men
and boys in the church, setting in groups on the
stone floor and making no end of noise—getting
their lessons by heart, Tom said, out of the Ko-
ran, which they think is a Bible, and people that
knows better knows enough to not let on. I never
see such a big church in my life before, and most
awful high, it was; it made you dizzy to look up;
our village church at home ain't a circumstance
to it; if you was to put it in there, people would
think it was a dry-goods box.

What I wanted to see was a dervish, because I
was interested in dervishes on account of the
one that played the trick on the camel driver. So
we found a lot in a kind of a church, and they
called themselves Whirling Dervishes; and they
did whirl, too. I never see anything like it. They

had tall sugar-loaf hats on, round and round like tops, and the petticoats stood out on a slant, and it was the prettiest thing I ever see, and made me drunk to look at it. They was all Moslems, Tom said, and when I asked him what a Moslem was, he said it was a person that wasn't Presbyterian. So there is plenty of them in Missouri, though I didn't know it before.

We didn't see half there was to see in Cairo, because Tom was in such a sweat to hunt out places that was celebrated in history. We had a most tiresome time to find the granary where Joseph stored up the grain before the famine, and when he found it it warn't worth much to look at, being such an old tumbledown wreck; but Tom was satisfied, and made more fuss over it than I would make if I struck a nail in my foot. How he ever found that place was too many for me. We passed as much as forty just like it before we came to it, and any of them would 'a' done for me, but none but just the right one would suit him; I never see anybody so particular as Tom Sawyer. The minute he stuck the right one he reconnized it as easy as I would reconnize my other shirt if I had one, but how he done it he couldn't any more tell than he could fly; he said so himself.

Then we hunted a long time for the house where the boy lived that learned the cadi how to try the case of the old olives and the new ones, and said it was out of the Arabian Nights, and he would tell me and Jim about it when he got time. Well, we hunted and hunted till I was ready to drop, and I wanted Tom to give it up and come next day and git somebody that knowed the town and could talk Missourian and could go straight to the place; but no, he wanted to find it himself, and nothing else would answer. So on we went. Then at last the remarkablest thing happened I ever see. The house was gone—gone hundreds of years ago—every last rag of it gone but just one mud brick. Now a person wouldn't ever believe that a backwoods Missouri boy that hadn't ever been in that town before could go and hunt that place over and find that brick, but Tom Sawyer done it. I know he done it, because I see him do it. I was right by his very side at the time, and see him see the bick and see him reconnize it. Well, I says to myself, how does he do it? Is it knowledge, or is it instink?"

Now there's the facts, just as they happened: let everybody explain it in their own way. I've ciphered over it a good deal, and it's my opinion that some of it is knowledge but the main bulk of it is instink. The reason is this: Tom put the brick in his pocket to give to a museum with his name on it and the facts when he went home, and I slipped it out and put another brick considerable like it in its place, and he didn't know the difference—but there was a difference, you see. I think that settles it—it's mostly instink, not knowledge. Instink tells him where the exact place is for the brick to be in, and so he reconnizes it by the place it's in, not by the look of the brick. If it was knowledge, not instink, he would know the brick again by the look of it the next time he seen it—which he didn't. So it shows that for all the brag you hear about knowledge being such a wonderful thing, instink is worth forty of the real unerringness. Jim says the same.

When we got back Jim dropped down and took us in, and there was a young man there with a red skullcap and tassel on and a beautiful silk jacket and baggy trousers with a shawl around his waist and pistols in it that could talk English and wanted to hire to us as guide and take us to Mecca and Medina and Central Africa and everywheres for a half a dollar a day and his keep, and we hired him and left, and piled on the power, and by the time we was through dinner we was over the place where the Israelites crossed the Red Sea when Pharaoh tried to overtake them and was caught by the waters. We stopped, then, and had a good look at the place, and it done Jim good to see it. He said he could see the Israelites walking along between the walls of water, and the Egyptians coming, from away off yonder, hurrying all they could, and see them start in as the Israelites went out, and then when they was all in, see the walls tumble together and drown the last man of them. Then we piled on the power again and rushed away and huvvered over Mount Sinai, and saw the place where Moses broke the tables of stone, and where the children of Israel camped in the plain and worshipped the golden calf, and it was all just as interesting as could be, and the guide knowed every place as well I knowed the village at home.

But we had an accident, now, and it fetched all the plans to a standstill. Tom's old ornery corn pipe had got so old and swelled and warped that she couldn't hold together any longer, notwithstanding the strings and bandages, but caved in and went to pieces. Tom he didn't know what to do. The professor's pipe wouldn't answer; it warn't anything but a mershum, and a person that's got used to a cob pipe knows it lays a long ways over all the pipes in this world, and you can't git him to smoke any other. He wouldn't take mine, I couldn't persuade him. So there he was.

He thought it over, and said we must scour around and see if we could roust out one in Egypt or Arabia or around in some of these countries, but the guide said no, it warn't no use, they didn't have them. So Tom was pretty glum for a little while, then he chirked up and said he'd got the idea and knowed what to do. He says:

"I've got another corncob pipe, and it's a prime one, too, and nearly new. It's laying on the rafter that's right over the kitchen stove at home in the village. Jim, you and the guide go and get

it, and me and Huck will camp here on Mount
Sinai till you come back."

"But, Mars Tom, we couldn't ever find de village. I could find de pipe, 'case I knows de
kitchen, but, my lan', we can't ever find de village, nur Sent Louis, nur none o' dem places.
We don't know de way, Mars Tom."

That was a fact, and it stumped Tom for a
minute. Then he said:

"Looky here, it can be done, sure; and I'll tell
you how. You set your compass and sail west as
straight as a dart, till you find the United States.
It ain't any trouble, because it's the first land
you'll strike the other side of the Atlantic. If it's
daytime when you strike it, bulge right on,
straight west from the upper part of the Florida
coast, and in an hour and three-quarters you'll
hit the mouth of the Mississippi—at the speed
that I'm going to send you. You'll be so high up
in the air that the earth will be curved considerable—sorter like a washbowl turned upside
down—and you'll see a raft of rivers crawling
around every which way, long before you get
there, and you can pick out the Mississippi without any trouble. Then you can follow the river

north nearly an hour and three-quarters, till you see the Ohio come in; then you want to look sharp, because you're getting near. Away up to your left you'll see another thread coming in— that's the Missouri and is a little above St Louis. You'll pass about twenty-five in the next fifteen minutes, and you'll recognize ours when you see it—and if you don't reckon you can yell down and ask."

"Ef it's dat easy, Mars Tom, I reckon we kin do it—yassir, I knows we kin."

The guide was sure of it, too, and thought that he could learn to stand his watch in a little while.

"Jim can learn you the whole thing in a half an hour," Tom said. "This balloon's as easy to manage as a canoe."

Tom got out the chart and marked out the course and measured it, and says:

"To go back west is the shortest way, you see. It's only about seven thousand miles. If you went east, and so on around, it's over twice as far." Then says to the guide, "I want you both to watch the telltale all through the watches, and whenever it don't mark three hundred miles an hour, you go higher or drop lower till you find a storm current that's going your way. There's a hundred miles an hour in this old thing without any wind to help. There's two-hundred-mile gales to be found, any time you want to hunt for them."

"We'll hunt for them, sir."

"See that you do. Sometimes you may have to go up a couple of miles, and it'll be p'ison cold, but most of the time you'll find your storm a good deal lower. If you can only strike a cyclone—that's the ticket for you! You'll see by the professor's books that they travel west in these latitudes; and they travel low, too."

Then he ciphered on the time, and says:

"Seven thousand miles, three hundred miles an hour—you can make the trip in a day—twenty-four hours. This is Thursday; you'll be back here Saturday afternoon. Come, now, hustle out some blankets and food and books and things for me and Huck, and you can start right along. There ain't no occasion to fool around—I want a smoke, and the quicker you fetch that pipe the better."

All hands jumped for the things, and in eight minutes our things was out and the balloon was ready for America. So we shook hands goodbye, and Tom gave his last orders:

"It's ten minutes to two P.M. now, Mount Sinai time. In twenty-four hours you'll be home, and it'll be six tomorrow morning, village time. When you strike the village, land a little back of the top of the hill, in the woods, out of sight; then you rush down, Jim, and shove these letters in the post office, and if you see anybody stirring, pull your slouch down over your face so they won't know you. Then you go and slip in the back way to the kitchen and git the pipe, and lay this piece of paper on the kitchen table, and put something on it to hold it, and then slide out and git away, and don't let Aunt Polly catch a sight of you, nor nobody else. Then you jump for the balloon and shove for Mount Sinai three hundred miles an hour. You won't have lost more than an hour. You'll start back at seven or eight A.M. village time, and be here in twenty-four hours, arriving at two or three P.M., Mount Sinai time."

Tom he read the piece of paper to us. He had wrote it:

*"THURSDAY AFTERNOON. Tom Sawyer
the Erronort sends his love to Aunt Polly
from Mount Sinai* where the Ark was, and
so does Huck Finn, and she will get it tomorrow morning half-past six.*

"TOM SAWYER THE ERRONORT."

"That'll make her eyes bulge out and the tears
come," he says. Then he says:

"Stand by! One—two—three—away you go!"

And away she did go! Why, she seemed to
whiz out of sight in a second.

Then we found a most comfortable cave that
looked out over the whole big plain, and there
we camped to wait for the pipe.

The balloon come back alright, and brung the
pipe; but Aunt Polly had catched Jim when he
was getting it, and anybody can guess what happened: she sent for Tom. So Jim he says:

"Mars Tom, she's out on de porch wid her eye
sot on de sky a-layin' for you, en she say she
ain't gwyne to budge from dah tell she gits hold

---

* This misplacing of the Ark is probably Huck's error, not
Tom's.—M. T.

of you. Dey's gwyne to be trouble, Mars Tom, 'deed dey is."

So then we shoved for home, and not feeling very gay, neither.